The Executioner was ready to die

Mack Bolan was trapped by enemy guns, alone against cutthroat competition.

A rifle bullet chipped the pavement by his elbow.

The Executioner looked in desperation for another angle of attack. Then he heard the welcome sound of April Rose's autorifle.

Together, in deadly tandem, they fired at the odds. Until horror hit hard like a bullet from hell.

And Mack Bolan watched as April Rose dropped, blood instantly staining the fabric of her jumpsuit....

Also available from Gold Eagle Books,
publishers of the Executioner series:

Mack Bolan's
ABLE TEAM

Mack Bolan's
PHOENIX FORCE

MACK BOLAN

THE EXECUTIONER 55

BOLAN

Paradine's Gauntlet

A GOLD EAGLE BOOK FROM

WORLDWIDE

TORONTO · NEW YORK · LONDON · PARIS
AMSTERDAM · STOCKHOLM · HAMBURG
ATHENS · MILAN · TOKYO · SYDNEY

First edition July 1983

ISBN 0-373-61055-6

Special thanks and acknowledgment to
Mike Newton for his contributions to this work.

Printed in Canada

"Against naked force the only possible defense is naked force. The aggressor makes the rules for such a war; the defenders have no alternative but to match destruction with more destruction, slaughter with greater slaughter."

—*Franklin D. Roosevelt*

"By extending the limits of the possible, I have tried to advance our thinking on the rules of war. But one thing never changes—it's either doing or dying, shoot or be shot."

—*Mack Bolan*

In memory of Lieutenant-Colonel Charles Robert Ray,
Assistant Military Attaché to the United States
Embassy in Paris, assassinated by gunmen
of the Armed Revolutionary Faction.

1

THE MAN CALLED HIMSELF LAVAL, and no one in the seamy world of waterfront Marseille had ever questioned that identity. Names were a matter of supreme indifference to his associates, men and women who could shed identities with the ease of changing clothes.

Laval was a businessman of renown along the southern coast of France, whose stock-in-trade was contraband: women, drugs or weapons—it mattered little to him. He was an opportunist. His customers served a purpose and Laval served them, as long as they had cash.

Business had been especially good of late. The Basques and Red Brigades were hungry for the weapons he could furnish, and a major deal for Turkish heroin was in the making with American buyers. Laval had never seen a better seller's market. He had never looked with such assurance to the future.

And then, last night . . . .

It was astonishing, the speed with which

disaster could materialize like a storm on the horizon, blotting out the progress of a lifetime. Without warning or explanation, Laval's house of cards had tumbled into ruins.

The fire had been catastrophic, raging through his warehouse, devouring heroin and hashish, detonating stockpiled ammunition. Two of his agents had been consumed by the flames, but Laval's interest lay only with his merchandise, with the incinerated inventory.

His customers would be suspicious, upset. He would be forced to reimburse them for their losses or replace the goods. Laval could deal with that; he could deal with the officials who would come with questions. He could deal with all of them...if only the fire had been an accident.

That was the problem.

It had not been an accident.

It had been an act of war.

Laval could easily shrug off the loss of the two employees, little more than glorified night watchmen, who had died inside the burning warehouse. But he could not accept so easily the other half dozen who had died outside, battling an enemy more lethal than the flames. He could see them in his mind: Pierre, his throat slit from ear to ear; and the others, huddled shells of flesh, bullet-torn, leaking blood in the fire's light. They were easily disposed of, but that did not eliminate the problem.

Laval had a war on his hands, and he was losing. The worst part it was that he did not even know the enemy's identity. You cannot fight if you do not know whom to fight, he thought. The assault was unexpected, unprecedented, devastating. Under the circumstances, there was only one intelligent course of action.

Laval was getting out.

Without believing anyone could really touch him, he had prepared himself for such an event. Any cautious businessman would do as much, insure himself against adversity. He kept a cache of U.S. dollars, Swiss francs and German marks ready for a flight into exile. The man had escape routes prepared in all directions.

At the moment, Laval was thinking of Algiers. He had connections there, and later, when the problems in Marseille had been resolved, he would return to pick up where he had left off. There would always be another time, but first he required a sanctuary.

Laval was certain that his monetary cache would be secure. No one knew about his safehouse, or about the sliding panel that concealed the vault within a walk-in closet.

The morning sky was breaking into dawn when he reached the safehouse. Laval was confident that no one saw him enter.

He was dead wrong.

Laval had been followed from the waterfront and traced to his lair by an enemy as grim as Death itself. The enemy, a soldier of the night, was waiting across the street, watching from the shadows as Laval emerged from the safehouse carrying a heavy suitcase. And that was all the soldier needed to see.

Mack Bolan had traveled 4,000 miles and killed eight men to get that view. He knew Laval on sight, although the face and name were strange to him forty-eight hours earlier. He recognized the enemy, and he knew what must be done.

Laval was on the shipping end of a narcotics pipeline that could flood America with heroin, enriching certain Eastern underworld chieftains in the process. Laval's nationality and the fortune he invested in police protection placed him well beyond the reach of law-enforcement agents from the States, but he was not beyond the reach of true justice. He was not protected from the action of The Executioner.

Laval had taken chances in his time, building a life for himself on the broken bodies and broken dreams of others. He was a cannibal, in debt far above his head to a universe that must be paid, and his note was coming due. The savage's account was being closed.

Laval hesitated on the steps, looking left and right, one hand buried in the pocket of his trench coat, the other weighted by the suitcase. A dozen strides would take him to the waiting Porsche and he would be away, running free and easy toward the airport and escape. An even dozen strides, and he would be safe.

Bolan slid the Beretta 93-R out of leather, testing its weight in his palm. A specially designed silencer would sacrifice something in muzzle velocity, but at a distance under twenty yards, neither marksman nor target would detect the difference.

Bolan took up his position at the curb.

Across the street, Laval was coming down the steps when he spotted Bolan. There was a flash of recognition in his eyes—for the situation rather than the man—and he reacted with the speed of one who has learned survival in the streets.

The Frenchman was gaining speed, almost reaching the Porsche as his right hand flashed out of his pocket clutching a pistol. Bolan recognized the Walther's flat report, buffeted back and forth between the sleeping houses, and he heard the whine of the bullet as it sliced air beside him, only inches off the mark. Laval was sacrificing accuracy in his haste.

Bolan tracked him with the 93-R, leading just enough to put the first round on target. He caressed the trigger and his weapon coughed in dignified response, a pencil line of flame lancing at the darkness. A single spent cartridge rattled on the pavement at his feet and rolled away.

The 9mm parabellum mangler took Laval in the heart, drilling flesh and bone, finding the vital pump then flattening against a shoulder blade. Its impact spun Laval. He died before his crashing corpse struck the fender of the Porsche.

Released from lifeless fingers, the suitcase sailed high before dropping, impacting on the sports car's shiny hood. The latches broke and the case sprang open like a giant clam, its contents freed. Bolan watched impassively as bundles of notes scattered across the street.

The universal debt was paid in full.

And Bolan's job was over. Another brush-fire skirmish in his endless war had ended with the savages suffering defeat and death. Weary of the hit-and-run, the monotony of kill or be killed, the warrior turned his thoughts toward home.

A brisk walk brought him to his waiting

rental car, and he put the street of death behind him.

Fifteen minutes and almost as many winding miles of narrow city streets brought him to a preselected curbside telephone. He left the sedan, moving quickly toward the lighted cubicle, scanning sparse traffic and deserted sidewalks with cautious eyes.

Bolan dropped a coin and dialed the special cut-out number, waiting as a complicated relay system patched him through to a clandestine office at the U.S. embassy in Paris. A young male voice answered on the third ring, phone lines humming softly as the scrambler automatically engaged.

"Yes."

It was neither question nor greeting.

"Phoenix, J.," he told the bland, impassive voice. "Code Omega, SM One. I'm coming in."

Hesitation at the other end.

"One moment, sir."

Bolan waited, uneasiness growing inside him, feeding on itself. A long, silent moment slipped away before a second, more mature voice came on the line.

"Sorry for the holdup, Phoenix. We've, uh, got a bit of a complication here."

Tension prickled at Bolan's scalp; knuckles whitened as he gripped the telephone receiver.

"Explain."

The desk jockey cleared his throat self-consciously before he answered.

"We have a telex out of D.C., Colonel. The message reads: 'Wonderland to Stony Man One. Rendezvous seaside at preassigned coordinates. Stand by for further contact soonest.' Shall I repeat?"

"Negative. Received and understood." Bolan disengaged, replacing the receiver without another word.

Yeah, he understood the message; he had prepared the code. In case of an emergency, he would remain afield and await instructions out of Washington.

Bolan knew the emergency was unrelated to his current mission. Laval was dead, the guy's heroin reduced to ash, the pipeline broken. Any rank-and-file survivors of the network would have to take their chances with the local law.

The job was finished in Marseille. It would be something else that required him to remain at large and prevented him from going home. He thought of the Blue Ridge Mountain country, and of Stony Man Farm, where he spent most of the brief moments of time between assignments.

Home.

Bolan shrugged it off. His real home was

on the firing line and in the trenches. Any other haven was illusory, a short bivouac between engagements with the enemy. Home was with the heart, and Mack Bolan's heart was dedicated to his endless war.

2

SARAH SHEPHERD, a tall, striking brunette, always opted for a window seat when flying, but today a layer of cloud obscured the Italian countryside below. They were still ninety minutes from touchdown, and she was tired, anxious to feel solid ground beneath her feet.

Sarah turned from the window, stifling a yawn. At thirty-two, she was probably the most important woman in the U.S. diplomatic service. Certainly, she had come further in the game than any other woman her age.

She was making it.

Underlying her jet lag and fatigue, Sarah felt an undeniable elation as she saw her long months of planning on the verge of paying off. From now on, it would be up to her superior, and she hoped he could nudge the last crucial pieces of the puzzle into place.

It had taken Sarah eight months of labor, working in conjunction with her Egyptian and Israeli counterparts, to make the meeting a reality. Sarah's superior would take the credit for it all, but she expected that. Still, she meant to get maximum mileage out of the conference.

It was not a formal summit conference, with premiers and presidents obliged to pose for photographs and answer questions from the media with vague generalities; it was a working summit, conducted by the men and women who get things done without the trappings of a carnival.

Sarah was one of four aides traveling with the U.S. Undersecretary of State from a preliminary meeting in North Africa. The other diplomats, Egyptian and Israeli, were supported by similar contingents—all presumably intent on bringing peace and order to the long-term chaos that had followed the Sadat assassination and the Israeli invasion of Lebanon. If they succeeded, they could change the bloody course of Middle Eastern history. If they failed . . . .

Any interference with the conference could prove disastrous. An international alliance was in charge of security around the meeting site in Switzerland.

The CIA and Secret Service were cooperating on security precautions for the flight, and everyone was aware that American prestige was on the line.

Sarah frowned, reflecting that professionally she was also on the line. Her superiors would be quick to cut their losses if the meeting fell through, and the ax would be falling close to home.

Movement in the center aisle distracted Sarah. She turned in time to see the chief of in-flight security as he passed by. Tall, blond and muscular, he moved with fluid grace, scanning the rows of seats in search of enemies. Grim-faced, eyes concealed behind the mirrored lenses of his aviator glasses, the man conveyed an aura of quiet menace.

Sarah watched him as he paused, conferring with one of his men beside the forward galley module. She wished all of them would make an effort to appear more unobtrusive and less sinister; they were steeped in the standard CIA mentality.

And yet Sarah felt the pervasive paranoia could be justified. The enemy was everywhere, and Switzerland's neutrality could not ensure a certain sanctuary for the peacemakers. There was always a need for guns and gunmen.

The thought depressed her, and Sarah put it out of her mind. Reclining in her seat, she closed her eyes and let the tension slip away. There was time to catch an hour's sleep before they landed. The soft vibration of the 747 carried her away.

THE MAN WITH THE BLOND HAIR turned away from his subordinate and continued toward the flight deck.

The men were ready, anxious to begin, and he did not want to keep them waiting. He shared their feeling of anticipation. This was his project, his obsession. Nothing could be allowed to stand in their way at the eleventh hour.

It had cost a small fortune to put his soldiers and himself aboard the 747. He had had to grease a hundred palms for information that would place the force within striking range.

Then the elimination of the first-string security team had been rapid. The bodies would be discovered soon—some of them might already be found, but it did not matter. There was no way to turn the flight around and abort the mission. They had passed the point of no return.

He reached the curving staircase and took the carpeted stairs two at a time, reaching the upper lounge where another of his men was standing watch. He acknowledged the sentry with a nod as he moved toward the cockpit door.

He slid a hand inside his jacket, feeling for the holstered Browning Hi-Power automatic, and a muscle twitched in his jaw as the new scar tissue underneath his arm pulled tight. The near-fatal bullet wound was fully healed, but the tenderness remained, a reminder of his brush with death—and of his great purpose.

The pain gave him focus.

The external pain and the icy rage inside him would both be eased when he achieved the revenge he sought against his enemies.

One enemy in particular.

He slipped through the cockpit door and pulled it shut behind him, sliding the automatic from its cross-draw holster. The Browning was cocked and locked; a flick of the safety lever with his thumb left the weapon primed to fire.

He had chosen special ammunition for his mission—the Browning held fourteen of the Blitz-Action-Trauma (BAT) rounds favored by the FBI and Secret Service. The 83-grain hollowpoints came with plastic nose plugs to ensure proper feed; the vented plug was blown away on firing, and would fall out of the screaming bullet's path.

The navigator and the first officer turned to face him, smiling in recognition. The captain, intent upon his instruments, did not see the pistol as it slid up and out to shoulder level. The blond man held the weapon steady, his eyes scanning behind the mirrored lenses.

"There has been a change in plan," he said.

The captain turned toward him for the first time, and his mouth dropped open as he saw the pistol. The first officer recovered first, his voice shaky as he spoke.

"What the hell's going on?"

"Our destination has been altered. We'll be turning east."

The captain found his voice, and with it something of his nerve.

"You don't want to use that thing in here," he cautioned. "Hit or miss, you're bound to cause explosive decompression— send us all right down the chute, yourself included."

The gunman swung the Browning slightly to the right, squeezing off a round as he made target acquisition.

The pistol roar was deafening in the confined space, expelling a hollowpoint at 1,400 feet per second. The slug impacted on his cheek below his left eye. At that range, the BAT projectile struck with 327 foot-pounds of energy, expanding to a massive .60 caliber, destroying everything before it. Face and skull imploded, and the copilot's lifeless form began its liquid slide toward the cockpit floor.

The BAT slug, designed with the protection

of bystanders in mind, spent its energy within the human target, and did not exit. No single fragment of the copper-nickel round escaped to damage windscreen or instruments.

The gunman swung the pistol back to a neutral point between the two surviving crew members.

"Now, if there are no further questions or objections . . . ."

He began speaking rapidly, snapping out directions and coordinates, taking charge. He was in control, and he planned to use the power that he held—with a vengeance.

3

"RENDEZVOUS SEASIDE at preassigned coordinates. Stand by for further contact soonest."

The coded order ran through Bolan's mind as he drove the Citroën sedan along the winding coastal highway. He was still puzzled by the order's sense of urgency, but there was no question in his mind about the designated point of rendezvous.

Every Phoenix mission—if possible—included built-in contingency plans, allowing for the unanticipated. Bolan approached each campaign with confidence, and with the realist's admission that anything could go wrong at any time. In the event of unforeseen disaster or diversion, he would be supplied with secondary systems of retreat and points of contact with his support troops.

In this mission he was heading for Six-Fours-la-Plage, a coastal town south of Toulon and twenty-five miles southeast of target zone Marseille.

He powered through the sleeping streets to-

ward the sea, past homes and shops where
the inhabitants had just begun to stir. He instinctively found the sea and nosed the
Citroën against a low retaining wall. He
killed the engine, set the brake and lit a cigarette.

In front of him, breakers tinted bloody by
the dawn were relentlessly rushing in toward
the sandy beach.

Bolan took a final drag on his cigarette and
flicked it out the window, shifting in his seat.
Movement in the rearview mirror had caught
his eye. He turned toward the source, automatically reaching for the silenced 93-R in its
armpit sheath. His cold blue eyes narrowed
into target recognition.

A long sleek motor home, painted gun-
metal blue with a gold stripe all around it,
was cruising along the beachfront road. He
had never seen the rig before, and yet there
was something very familiar about it.

Bolan kept his hand wrapped around the
cool Beretta as the big motor home turned off
the pavement, rumbled over gravel in the
parking lot and slowed to a halt against the
seawall twenty yards to his left. The driver
and any passengers were invisible behind
smoked glass.

A door slid open on the vehicle's starboard
side. Nothing had prepared him for the sight

of the figure that appeared in the doorway.

Four thousand miles from home, standing in the first light of dawn, April Rose looked as beautiful as he had ever seen her. Her sparkling eyes met and locked with his. Her smile was hesitant, expectant.

He got out of the car, moved toward her and swept her into a strong embrace. April's warmth and softness reminded Bolan of another life—one worth fighting for, and dying for.

"Sorry about the red alert, Striker."

Bolan turned toward the familiar voice and found Hal Brognola framed in the open doorway of the motor home. The big Fed's smile was weary, and as usual he looked like a man with bad news on his mind.

Bolan returned the smile and moved toward his old friend, April Rose following in lock-step, holding his arm.

"Nice wheels," he said. "I didn't know you were the nostalgic type."

Brognola shrugged.

"Just a little something we threw together. Come aboard."

Bolan mounted the folding steps with April in tow, and the dark blue door slid shut behind them. He scanned the roomy interior, taking in the banks of electronic hardware with workshop and living quarters in the rear.

The warrior was impressed, and he did not try to hide it.

"It feels like home," Bolan said.

Hal grinned.

"She's got everything you had on the original, and then some," the man from Washington, D.C., replied. "Our friends have added all the latest laser weaponry and optics."

Bolan experienced an overwhelming sense of déjà vu. He had owned such a vehicle in another life, and he had ridden it to victory in phase one of his war against the cannibals.

Constructed by aerospace engineers and dubbed a "terrain module," the prototype had first seen action in his death struggle with the New Orleans troops of *Don* Marco Vannaducci. From there, it had served him well in a dozen other campaigns against the Mafia.

And finally, with April Rose at the helm, the War Wagon saw him through his bloody six-day "Second Mile" against the mob. Its fiery self-destruction on a rainy Sunday afternoon in Central Park had paved the way for Bolan's own rebirth as Colonel John Phoenix.

Memories.

The new war machine was a twenty-six-foot GMC motor home with extras the designers in Detroit had never dreamed of. As modified by Stony Man technicians, it was self-contained, a battlefield command center that was virtually as mobile as the man himself. With a 450-cubic-inch power plant beneath the hood, front traction and the tandem rear wheels with air-bag suspension, the vehicle was capable of both evasion and pursuit. A secondary generator handled all unique electrical requirements of the combat systems.

Conventional wraparound windows had been supplanted by a system of replaceable panels with strategically positioned one-way-vision portholes. Amidships, the mobile war room featured a central combat-scenario command console whose computerized functions could be performed by remote control from the forward deck when he was driving. The weapons lab and armory provided ample storage space for weapons and munitions; the living quarters aft included toilet, shower and folding bunks for four.

The heart of the electronic intelligence-gathering unit employed computerized selection and switching circuits built to handle radio pickups, plus sensitive audio and optic scanners that functioned within the telemetry systems being fed into the console for synchronizing, editing and sorting, time-phasing, re-recording and microstoring of accumulated data.

The navigation system utilized a "shared-time" concept with the other electronics, allowing for complete instrument control in zero-visibility surroundings. Hidden rocketry provided Bolan with a heavy-punch capability. The system operated from the driver's seat with night-bright optics, laser-supplemented infrared illuminators, and with an automatic target acquisition via audio and video sensors.

The system could also be operated by remote control for extra-vehicular activity, allowing Bolan even greater combat stretch.

And those were just the features he could see, the ones he knew about. If Hal had turned the government designers loose, with all the laser weaponry available today...the potential was nothing short of awesome.

It was not just the War Wagon anymore. It was a new sophisticated Laser Wagon—with horsepower, firepower, *striking* power.

He found a seat at the communications console and April settled in beside him. Hal Brognola was watching him intently, and Bolan broke the ice.

"We're a long way from the showroom. What's the action, Hal?"

Brognola's mouth turned downward in a scowl as he answered.

"The action's Paradine."

Bolan was stunned. The name recalled vivid images of carnage on a Turkish battlefield early in his terrorist wars. Bolan had believed that the mercenary known as Paradine was dead. But apparently he had been mistaken.

"Go on."

Brognola cleared his throat and started from the top.

"Paradine has picked off a diplomatic flight en route to Switzerland. He's got a dozen hostages, plus crew. There were Americans aboard, with Egyptians and Israelis, bound for a top-secret summit on the Middle East."

"Sponsorship?" Bolan asked.

Hal shook his head.

"No intelligence available. Defense suspects the Soviets, or any one of a half-dozen Arab splinter groups. All of them would profit from disruption of the talks. Who knows, Paradine could be going independent."

"Are they down?"

"The plane was found abandoned near the village of Tolmezzo in Italy, near the Yugoslav border. Nervy bastard put it down on a highway, if you can picture that. Landed on the only long stretch of straight tarmac for hundreds of miles around. The man himself has got to be in the vicinity."

"What's the going price these days?"

Brognola's scowl deepened.

"I'll let you listen for yourself. We found this tape aboard the plane...beside a murdered member of the crew."

He plugged a cassette into the console, adjusting the volume as blank leader tape hissed through the wall-mounted speakers. Another moment, and a cold, atonal voice surrounded them.

"This is Paradine. As leader of the People's Revolutionary Front, I have taken into custody the representatives of three imperialist nations. They will each be executed if their governments do not concede to the following demands within forty-eight hours.

"First, they will arrange for the release of certain soldiers of the people's army, presently incarcerated inside the Turkish and West German police states. Names and all particulars shall be transmitted at a later time.

"Next, they will deliver one billion dollars' worth of flawless gem-quality diamonds to the place that I direct, as partial reparations for their exploitation of the masses."

Paradine's voice hesitated, letting that demand sink in, and when he spoke again the voice had grown even chillier.

"Delivery of the diamonds shall be made by the agent code-named Phoenix. This is nonnegotiable. If he is unavailable, evidence of death must be presented with the reparations payment. His head will be acceptable.''

April Rose shivered perceptibly. Bolan sat impassively, waiting for the disembodied voice to finish.

"Acceptance of these terms should be communicated hourly until received on Radio Free Europe. Delivery instructions will then be telephoned to the U.S. embassy in Paris. All power to the people."

Momentary silence reigned inside the van, broken finally by Bolan.

"Any thoughts on how he made the name?"

"Negative, Striker. They're climbing walls around the Oval Office, but so far everybody checks out clean. My best guess would be a rumble in the underground, maybe a survivor with a grudge and a tale to tell. He can't know anything for certain."

"He knows too much, Hal!" April snapped. "If we bite on this, we'll be jeopardizing everything."

Bolan felt the tension between Hal and April, and he realized that they were in the middle of an ongoing argument. He took April's hand, addressing her directly.

"No way to pass it up," he told her. "I should have done it right the first time."

Brognola cleared his throat.

"I knew you'd see it that way," he said. "We sent the word at three o'clock this morning."

"Any feedback?"

"It's confirmed," Hal answered. "They want to check you out, make sure that you're alone and all that. Paradine plans to walk you through some checkpoints before delivery's finalized. There's a contact waiting in Monaco, and you'll get the rest from him. I have the details for you when you're ready."

"What's the time frame?"

"Tight and counting. We've used a quarter of those forty-eight hours already."

"No time to waste, then."

"Well, Striker, I thought you might find some use for the battle buggy here. Take it on a little shakedown cruise, you know?"

"Too conspicuous," Bolan said. "The shakedown will have to wait."

Brognola seemed about to argue when April chimed in, taking Bolan's side.

"He's right, Hal. We need to keep a low profile. The two of us—"

Bolan cut her off.

"Forget it, April. No room for passengers this time around."

Her eyes flashed with anger.

"I can pull my weight and you know it,"

she said. "You're going to need all the help you can get with that animal waiting for you."

"Not this time," he repeated, soft but firm.

April stared hard at him, fists clenched. "Dammit!" she said as she stormed out of the Laser Wagon, sliding the door shut loudly behind her.

Bolan watched her go, remembering the times when they had fought together, side by side against the savages. The lady could pull her weight and then some. But he refused to risk her life.

Hal's voice distracted him from private thoughts.

"You just kicked a hornet's nest, guy. I'm going to catch hell for this."

Bolan managed a weary smile.

"You can take the heat," he said, "and she'll get over it. Let's get down to business."

Ten minutes later, selected ordnance and a heavy satchel full of diamonds had been transferred from the wagon to Bolan's Citroën. He had memorized directions and coordinates for his first checkpoint.

With the transfer completed, two old friends spent a parting moment. Hal shook hands with Bolan and wished him well in a solemn voice, clearly reluctant to see him go.

"Watch this bastard, Mack," he cautioned. "He's got a hate for you that won't quit, and he meant that crack about your head on a platter."

"I'll watch it," Bolan said.

Hal nodded, left him by the Citroën, then disappeared inside the motor home. Bolan was turning toward the rented car when April reappeared beside him, reaching out to touch his arm. Her eyes were moist, but her voice was firm.

"You're making a mistake, soldier."

April saw that her man could not be swayed from his decision.

"Hey... I love you," she told him.

Bolan smiled and pulled her close.

4

BOLAN GUNNED THE CITROEN along the coastal highway. Intent upon his mission, he ignored the beautiful view of the Mediterranean. He would leave the scenery to the tourists.

The man called Paradine was a living mystery—only sketchy information about him existed in the Stony Man files. Bolan's team possessed a composite likeness of the man, constructed from a knowledge of his physical dimensions, and his age was estimated to be thirty-five. The rest was blank—no photographs or fingerprints available, no date of birth or nationality. Nothing, except for the bloody trail he left behind.

Paradine was a mercenary terrorist, offering his lethal talents to the highest bidder without regard to politics or creed. Despite persistent stories of liaison with the Soviets, he never seemed to serve the same cause twice. His name had been connected with a dozen of the worst terrorist atrocities in a decade marked by ceaseless revolutionary warfare. Rumor placed him in the neighborhood of a grisly massacre in Rome, the demolition of the U.S. embassy in Beirut, Lebanon, the sniper slayings of American diplomats in Paris. The list went on.

Bolan had seen the bastard twice—at the scene of a massacre in Beverly Hills, and again at a training center for the Turkish People's Liberation Army, in the rugged Kara Mountain country. The Executioner had scuttled Paradine's designs on the latter occasion and attempted to kill the terrorist.

There had not been any time to confirm the kill. Evidently Paradine had lived. Bolan was determined not to miss a second time.

Experience had taught him that a viper will retain its lethal potency until the venom-bearing head is severed and obliterated. So it was with evil. Paradine cared nothing for the soldiers in his ''people's army,'' neither those Bolan killed nor the survivors rotting in their prison cells. His demand for their release was a sham, obligatory window dressing, disguise for his primary purpose. Even the ransom payment, while significant, would be secondary in the terrorist's mind.

Delivery of the diamonds was simply a

device to place the living target within range, to let Paradine avenge the pain and humiliation of their Turkish encounter.

Bolan did not know his enemy, but he knew the type. Stoic in the heat of battle, Paradine would be relentless in pursuit of vengeance to soothe his wounded ego.

The lion's share of Paradine's destructive energy would be channeled toward retaliation for its own sake, a compulsion to get even, to destroy and humiliate the object of his rage. He would never rest until he paid Phoenix back for the defeat in Turkey, or until he died.

Vengeance was a pitiful motive to Mack Bolan. Anyone who spent their campaigns avenging every defeat would continue to lose. Anytime whatsoever spent in jealously avenging losses and humiliations was time ill spent. Such time would eat at the future with all the corrosive rust of the past, and no progress could be made—only further failure.

Bolan would be acting from very different motives. He had to free the hostages, and he had to rid the world of a certified monster, to destroy the viper's head and its rotten body.

His were forward-looking motives. Paradine was a job unfinished, incomplete, and Bolan never did anything halfway. He was going for scorched earth, total destruction of the mercenary terrorist. The warrior would succeed this time, or he would spend all his blood in the attempt.

"I DON'T CARE WHAT HE SAID," April snapped. "He needs help, even if he won't admit it."

Hal Brognola watched her through the haze of smoke rising from his cigar.

"Is that the head talking, or the heart?"

April frowned.

"They go together," April insisted. "Listen, Hal, you know Mack feels responsible for Paradine. He won't rest until he makes it right."

"That's the job, April," he reminded her.

"Where's it written that he has to do it alone?"

Brognola scowled around his cigar. "How do you plan to find him?"

"I know as much about the first rendezvous coordinates as he does. If I miss him there, well—I planted a homer in the Citroën. I can trail him from a distance if I have to."

Hal shook his head. "He isn't going to like it," he said.

"I'll take that chance." She hesitated, gauging Hal's reaction. "There's one thing you can do to help."

"What's that?"

"Take a taxi home."

He blew another plume of smoke toward the ceiling, holding his temper. "Have you really thought this through?"

She nodded grimly. "All the way."

April Rose had met Mack Bolan for the first time on the Monday of his week-long "Second Mile" against the Mafia. She had fought with Hal then too, resisting her assignment as the warrior's driver and technical support. Back then, April had disapproved of Bolan, ethically and personally, in spite of the strong physical attraction that she could not deny.

Bloody Monday altered April's thinking irreversibly. By the end of that first day, Bolan had not only saved her life, but changed it. She had passed through the fire and emerged with a commitment to the man and to his cause, if they were ever separable. When the Phoenix team was constituted, April was the first aboard; nothing short of death could have kept her off the squad and away from Bolan's side.

And if some might confuse her dedication to the man with love, April would not argue. She loved the warrior with her body and her soul, receiving an equal measure in return.

She loved the man too much, in fact, to

obey his orders now, too much to let him run the gauntlet alone. April Rose was backing Mack Bolan.

All the way.

5

THE BLACK MERCEDES circled the block, cruising slowly like a hungry shark. Reconnaissance complete, the driver parked against the curb outside the Café Justine, a weathered waterfront establishment.

The restaurant was a favorite nocturnal haven for the underworld figures of Nice, but daylight was cruel to the café. It exposed it for what it was—an ancient whore, stripped of all mystery and allure.

The Mercedes disgorged a pair of carbon-copy hardmen. One of them lingered by the car while his partner took the point, scanning the street and sidewalk. When he was satisfied, the scout took up his post beside the café entrance.

Another man emerged from the Mercedes, smartly dressed in a pearl gray business suit. He crossed the sidewalk and passed inside, the hardguys trailing. The guncocks followed their boss across the dark interior and left him only when he gained the stairs, peeling off on either side to close the way.

Upstairs, a somber trio waited for the new arrival in a smoky conference room. An empty chair was waiting at the head of the table, and the newcomer filled it with his bulk.

He was called Louis, and as the ranking leader of the *Union Corse*, he was given due respect. A scarred and grizzled veteran of the Riviera drug wars, he had alternately fought and worked with mafiosi, Communists and American intelligence. Since the death of the American intruder, "Monzoor" Rudolfi, Louis had risen rapidly to stand astride the underworld of southern France. He owed that rise, and the commensurate advancement of his brother Corsicans, to his own ferocity and to the timely intervention of *L'Américaine Formidable*, now also happily deceased. In a jungle full of savages, Louis was the strongest, most tenacious of the tribe.

He addressed the eldest of his three lieutenants, a balding, one-eyed survivor of the streets and gutters who had risen in Louis's shadow to the pinnacles of power. Louis's voice rumbled up from deep inside his barrel chest.

"What news from the Sûreté?"

"My people are in touch with the Americans. The ransom will be paid."

Louis nodded. "Continue."

"As you know, the demand requires delivery by one man. We should have no difficulty in relieving him of the goods."

"No difficulty," Louis repeated, "if they follow their instructions to the letter. We must learn the time and place."

"Monaco."

Louis cocked an eyebrow at his friend.

"Confirmation?"

"Positive."

The Corsican smiled.

"Prepare the family. Make every soldier understand our top priority."

He fanned the air with one hand, a gesture of dismissal. In another moment he was left alone.

Louis relaxed and lit a cigarette, trying to imagine one billion dollars' worth of diamonds. He would lose sixty cents on every dollar in the fencing process, but the profit would still be close to 200 million francs. A fortune, and badly needed at the moment.

That very morning, he had learned of Laval's assassination in Marseille and the destruction of important heroin reserves. Sinister and inexplicable, the sudden violence might foreshadow open war within the underworld, accompanied by harassment from authorities. Louis was anxious to recoup his losses, fatten up his war chest before the shooting started. Forty million francs would help the *Union* withstand a lengthy siege.

Louis was ready to lead his troops to Monaco.

GIOVANNI GORO CHECKED THE ACTION of his Walther P-38 and left the safety off as he returned it to his belt. It was small enough protection, but the young man was pressed for time and there had been no chance to secure other arms on his way to the urgent rendezvous.

He risked a glance around the corner, briefly exposing his body at the alley's mouth, quickly ducking back under cover. Everything looked normal at a glance, the way it had in Naples three weeks before. He had not seen a trace of the SIG commandos before they opened fire, blasting out of second-story windows, spraying bullets from a van parked against the curb. Two close friends had fallen, riddled in the cross fire, and only Giovanni Goro had escaped. Disgusted, he attributed his own survival not to skill or planning, but to plain dumb luck.

There had been enough luck in recent times, most of it bad. As a captain in the Red Brigades, Goro was accustomed to the element of risk, but ever since the Dozier debacle, he felt he was on the verge of losing control.

Pressure from the Special Police Corps' Security Central Operation, and worse, from the paramilitary Special Intervention Group, was relentless.

Hard-eyed gunmen of the SIG were everywhere, scouring the underground for Red Brigades stragglers, shooting first and asking questions only when the body count was taken. Brigades prestige was at an all-time low, the coffers dangerously close to empty as the heat dried up secret sources of support.

Weapons were expensive, and because of the escalating danger, potential recruits had grown reluctant to enlist without considerable financial compensation. It repulsed Goro to involve himself with mercenaries, but he was a realist and a veteran of the urban struggle, willing to use anyone, any tool, in furtherance of holy revolution.

Lately, however, he had considered getting out, but his clandestine travel agent had been traced to Rome and shot while trying to evade police. Goro was evaluating other options, seeking other means of escape, when his luck began to change. An opportunity was handed to him, ripe and ready for the picking. All he had to do was get across the street alive.

The target was a cheap hotel, separated

from the alleyway by twenty yards of open pavement. It should have been secure—his agent in Milan had guaranteed safe passage—but the same had been true in Naples. Twenty yards could stretch forever if the SIG was waiting for him, in a car with engine idling, or in the windows overhead. Twenty yards could be a lifetime.

Goro braced himself, one hand on the Walther as he crossed the street, eyes fixed upon the hotel entrance.

He made it in a walk, beginning to relax only when he reached the lobby. He kept his fingers wrapped around the pistol as he by-passed an ancient elevator in favor of the stairs. Two flights up he reached his destination. He rapped out a coded signal on the numbered door.

The door opened to reveal a sallow face, Goro's local contact, Vito Lettieri. Shifty rodent's eyes examined him, then peered around his shoulder, checking out the corridor beyond. When he was satisfied, Lettieri stood aside and let the new arrival pass.

Inside the dingy room, another man was seated at an old dining table, watching closely. The stubby muzzle of his submachine gun, a Beretta Model 12, followed Goro like an extra sightless eye until the man made the recognition and laid the gun aside. Goro took a seat across from him, and Lettieri settled on his left, having stopped for some wine and glasses on the way. He filled a glass and passed the bottle, offering a crooked, mirthless smile.

"Schroeder sends his compliments," the ferret said.

Goro frowned. The German, a member of the Baader-Meinhof gang, was hiding in the south of France and waiting for officials to forget his face at home. They had worked together in the past, and it was Schroeder who had leaked the word to Lettieri of a major project in progress.

"What else does he send?"

"Good news," Lettieri answered. "The Americans will pay."

"Is the landing verified?"

Lettieri nodded once. "Outside Tolmezzo."

"And the border?"

"We're in touch. They didn't cross."

"Very well. The delivery will be made on Italian soil." He pinned Lettieri with a penetrating stare. "We need the time and place."

Lettieri frowned, dropped his eyes and stared at the bottom of his wineglass.

"I'm working on it now," he said.

"Work harder. This is your assignment. If you fail. . . ."

Goro left the statement hanging. Lettieri's own imagination filled the gap, and there was fear behind the eyes when finally he raised his head.

"You'll have it, don't worry. My people are reliable."

"I hope so. We cannot afford another failure."

He rose, and turned his back on Lettieri and the silent gunner. Goro felt their eyes upon him as he reached the door. He hesitated with a hand on the knob. He pivoted to face his rodent-faced lieutenant.

"Two hours, Vito. Have the information when I call again."

And he left them, slipping out and moving toward the stairs before either of them had a chance to answer. Automatically, instinctively, he scanned the corridor, alert to any sudden sound or movement.

Lettieri would not fail, he was sure of that. Ruthless and efficient, he would follow orders out of fear, if nothing else. Fear was Giovanni Goro's business, and he knew its value as a motivator.

As he hit the stairs, Goro had his mind on money. One billion U.S. dollars translated into nearly sixty-five billion lire...enough wealth to help the Red Brigades regain lost ground and start looking toward the future.

In a single stroke they could eclipse the score of other splinter factions operating around the Mediterranean, and assume preeminence among European terrorists.

Giovanni Goro smiled at the thought of undercutting Paradine, robbing him of gold and glory. He had met the mercenary twice and remembered him as cold, evasive. Goro had mistrusted him as he mistrusted every gun for hire. It would be a pleasure to disrupt his master plan and take the legendary warrior down a peg or two.

The euphoric mood evaporated as he reached the lobby, heading for the open street. All his hopes were resting now on Vito Lettieri and his network of informers. If they obtained the information he required, if he, Giovanni, could evade authorities and pull his troops together at the target site, if the ransom was delivered, they would have a chance.

First, he would have to keep himself alive for two more hours.

IVAN ILLYANOVICH CLOSED THE THICK manila folder and rested his massive hands on top of it. He glanced around the Spartan office, eyes settling on the framed pictures of Lenin, Marx, and Uri Andropov. The latter, a new addition in a narrow frame, was slightly smaller than the portrait of Leonid Brezhnev, which it had replaced. Faded paint was visible around the edges, and Illyanovich decided he would speak with maintenance soon. At the moment, there were other pressing problems on his mind—all of them concerning the adventures of the man called Paradine.

The placard on his office door proclaimed Illyanovich to be Assistant Cultural Attaché. In fact, he was a section chief of *Komitet Gosudarstvennoi Bezopasnosti* (KGB) and as such, the single most important figure at the Soviet embassy in Belgrade. His responsibilities included state security, disinformation, espionage and certain other delicate assignments that required a screen of strict deniability—such as sponsorship of terrorism in the West, a role Illyanovich embraced with special fondness.

The *Komitet* had sponsored Paradine before, lending guidance and support through an elaborate buffer network. Even now, an agent was planted in his entourage, feeding information back whenever possible, but the control was slipping. Since the Turkish operation fell apart in flames, Paradine had been dangerously independent and erratic. He had all the earmarks of a maverick, and his latest action had been undertaken free of sponsorship.

The hijacking did not faze Illyanovich; any interruption of the Middle Eastern peace talks was welcome. If the hostages should die, and thus precipitate another war, so much the better. Such an outcome would escalate the sale of arms and broaden Soviet influence with the Arab nations.

No, it was not the operation, but rather Paradine's obsession with personal revenge that Illyanovich found disconcerting. It implied that Paradine was losing touch with the realities of his profession, sacrificing objectivity and putting everything at risk. It would be regrettable to lose an operative of his potential, and yet. . . .

Illyanovich reflected that Paradine's fixation with the Western agent Phoenix might be turned to Soviet advantage. The section chief had lately been preoccupied with a disturbing trend in terrorist affairs—the disruption of paramilitary groups and operations by an unknown hand, striking hard and deep at the eleventh hour.

Thus far, covert actions had been scuttled, with the loss of valued personnel in Colombia, West Germany, Algiers, Italy, Nicaragua, in the United States itself. . . not to mention Paradine's own spectacular fiasco in Turkey. Other nagging rumors had a special agent doing costly damage in the satellite countries—Libya, Iran and Vietnam. There were few survivors, but the name Phoenix had surfaced more than once, and Illyanovich was no believer in coincidence.

Skeptical of one man's ability to wreak such havoc, the Central Committee had discouraged any mass effort to identify him and his death squads. Ivan had dissented, quietly, of course, but his covert inquiries had been frustrated by a veil of secrecy and death. Despite his conviction that the Phoenix agent and his neutralization squads must be either British or American, Illyanovich's efforts to pin him down, to get a handle on his whereabouts and movements, had failed.

Now, thanks to Paradine, the *Komitet* might have a shot at Phoenix. If the man existed. If he dared respond to Paradine's demand.

If.

Elimination of the Phoenix secret weapon was a goal to be urgently pursued. Success would be a major coup, strategically and individually. Best of all, Illyanovich could claim full credit, flying in the face of party apparatus denials. It might even be enough to take him home, back to Moscow and the heart of the action.

If it all fell through, well, Ivan Illyanovich was a survivor, an expert at covering his tracks, cutting his losses. Deniability was the order of the day, every day.

He punched a button on the desk-top intercom, and a moment later his lieutenant entered. Stern-faced and humorless, young Protopkin was the only man Illyanovich could trust implicitly inside the embassy.

"Call Nosenko," he instructed. "Have him here within the hour."

Protopkin nodded silently and left. The door clicked firmly shut behind him.

Alone again, Ivan Illyanovich relaxed, rocking back in his recliner chair to wait, pondering which shade of gray to order for the walls.

6

EUROPE'S PLAYGROUND is the French Riviera,
and the Riviera's pulsing heart is Monaco.
Roughly two square kilometers in area, the
tiny principality exists to serve the self-
proclaimed Beautiful People. Revenues from
the casino at Monte Carlo are sufficient to
help exempt the 30,000 inhabitants from tax-
ation. The casino is government-controlled,
and Monaco is spared the taint of syndicate
involvement found in Las Vegas, Atlantic
City and the Caribbean.

Even so, there were savages in evidence;
the Mediterranean was full of hungry
sharks.

Mack Bolan had come to France the first
time as a fugitive, spinning off from his early
clashes with the Mafia at home. He was looking for a refuge, a sanctuary. What he found
was another battlefront. The Mafia was eating France alive, and the resident *capo*,
Thomas "Monzoor" Rudolfi, was master of
ceremonies at the feast. Bolan's head-on col-

lision with the cannibals had been inevitable, preordained.

Warrior Bolan took the first swings, and Rudolfi, his reputation on the line, employed a desperate gambit. Ten women, courtesans from a *maison de joie*, were taken hostage in exchange for *L'Américaine Formidable*. Ten lives for the price of one, with Bolan's fate and that of France hanging in the balance. The Executioner responded with audacity and daring, delivering an ultimatum.

For every hour that the women were in jeopardy, one ranking member of the underworld would die...and die they did. The final target fell in Monaco, inside the casino itself, before Rudolfi saw the light. Cornered by police and mafiosi, Bolan had escaped with the aid of unexpected allies, blitzing on to execute Rudolfi.

Now, the Executioner was returning to Monaco. There were still serpents in the garden, still hostages in jeopardy.

Bolan crossed into Monaco at 10:00 A.M.

He passed the casino, already crowded in spite of the early hour, then headed south, winding down the remarkable streets for which the resort was renowned, and which had claimed the life of its famous American princess, down toward the harbor and his designated rendezvous. Circling the marina parking lot, he found a space for the Citroën and backed into it. Bolan did not want any complications if he had to quit the harbor in a hurry.

The warrior prepared himself to go EVA. He double-checked the Beretta's load, returned it to leather, and fished a yellow silk scarf out of the glove compartment. The scarf would serve as a recognition signal.

He left the satchel full of diamonds with his military hardware, locked securely in the Citroën's trunk. Bolan put his trust in the Beretta 93-R, and in his certainty that Paradine would not be anxious to provoke a public firefight. The mercenary wanted Bolan to himself.

Bolan reached the pier and continued on, mingling with tourists. Unbidden, his mind recalled another walk along that pier, with a score of gunners waiting for him, fingers itching on the triggers. He had survived that gauntlet and now returned, this time to face a single man.

The warrior found a place against the railing, and stared off across the sunlit water. He felt a man beside him, at his elbow.

"The sea is beautiful," the man said.

"But cold and cruel," Bolan answered.

Password completed, Bolan turned to face the new arrival. His contact was average size and build, with a pock-marked face and sandy hair worn long over ears and collar. The pistol in its shoulder rig was obvious beneath the O.D. fatigue jacket. Denim jeans and paratrooper's boots completed the picture.

"Let's walk," the contact said.

Bolan fell into step beside the man, moving out along the pier.

"Where's Paradine?" Bolan asked.

"Waiting for you," his contact answered. "First, he wants to make certain his demands are met. You have the diamonds?"

Bolan nodded, then growled, "I deliver them to Paradine, or not at all."

"Understood. You were told to come alone."

Bolan glanced around and said, "I don't see any reinforcements."

"We've arranged some precautions. You'll be passed through a series of checkpoints like this. In between, you'll be observed. Any contact or delay you cannot explain will sacrifice the hostages."

"How do I know they're still alive?"

"You don't. Your next checkpoint is in Chiasso." The contact checked his wristwatch. "It's around 170 miles. Call it four hours from the time I make the call. Someone will be waiting for you off the square."

Bolan nodded, turned and left. He reached his Citroën and slid behind the wheel. Paradine's man had vanished by the time he cranked the engine into life. Bolan wheeled out of the parking lot toward the open road.

Five minutes later, he recognized the tail. A red Peugeot was hanging tight, changing lanes a mere beat behind the Citroën. Bolan counted four men sandwiched into the compact, hard eyes staring at him.

Bolan took the car around the block, and by the time he merged again with mainstream traffic, a Fiat had fallen in behind the Peugeot. Call it eight guns, minimum, clinging to his track.

He ticked off the possibilities, discarding each in turn. Brognola would never stick him with a tail, but there were other players. The Egyptians and Israelis both had lives at stake; either side might attempt to monitor the drop and take revenge against the terrorists. The Mossad especially was capable of picking up the challenge, but....

Bolan shrugged off the thought. Any secret service that could penetrate Brognola's Stony Man security could also run an unobtrusive tail. The gunners on his track were clumsy in their eagerness, edging closer, not trying to conceal themselves.

He thought of Paradine. It was conceivable

the terrorist would try to suck him in, walk him through a setup rendezvous and then pick him off with his defenses down. In that event, Bolan knew his enemy would be among the trackers, or waiting close at hand, ready to administer the killing stroke.

He gunned the Citroën, cutting hard across two lanes of traffic, breaking off from the main drag. Behind him, a screech of brakes and the clamor of protesting horns reported that the tail was hanging on. That was fine with Bolan, but he did not want to engage the enemy with innocent civilians in the cross fire.

His first preference would be to shake the trackers. Failing that, the Executioner would stand and fight, but on a killing ground of his choice, where the danger to civilians could be minimized.

Bolan headed northeast through a neighborhood of smaller shops and restaurants.

Suddenly, someone in the Peugeot got anxious, started feeling for the range with semi-automatic fire.

The first round struck Bolan's trunk, caroming into empty space.

He checked the mirror and saw the tail cars bristling with weaponry. Steady fire was crackling from the Peugeot, and gunners in the Fiat, momentarily obstructed by the point car, were looking for a field of fire.

Bolan weaved back and forth across the center stripe, throwing off the gunners' aim. Driving one-handed, he reached under the seat. He freed the Uzi mini-submachine gun from its harness and laid it beside him.

The mini-Uzi was a severely cut-down version of the classic Israeli submachine gun. With the metal stock folded, it measured an incredible 9.5 inches shorter than the parent weapon, and a full inch shorter than the Ingram M-10 machine pistol. Designed with concealment in mind, the stubby man-shredder nevertheless sacrificed none of its antecedent's firepower, rivaling the full-grown Uzi in velocity, rate of fire and stopping power. Thirty-two 9mm parabellum steel-jackets nestled in the staggered-box magazine. A broom-handle arrangement of vertical magazines could be used to escalate the number of rounds dramatically.

Bolan had his weapon and his target; all he needed was the killing ground. And if he did not find it soon, the gunners on his tail might start getting lucky.

A side street appeared on the right. Bolan swung hard, making it on two wheels, the squat sedan rocking into touchdown as he cleared the corner. Behind him, the Peugeot's driver missed the turn, standing on his brakes and smoking rubber as the Fiat cut across his track to follow Bolan. For the first time, gunners in the Fiat opened fire.

Running ahead of the hounds, Bolan was opening the throttle, looking for some combat stretch.

Then he saw his error: he had picked a cul-de-sac, and ahead of him, the street was sealed off tight by a solid wall of brick and native stone.

The Executioner was boxed in, gunners at his back, hurtling on a collision course with stone at sixty miles an hour.

7

LOUIS, THE CORSICAN, had hoped to take the ransom payment from his solitary target with a minimum of violence. He was not opposed to killing and did not expect his quarry to surrender voluntarily, but at the same time he dreaded any thought of open battle in the streets of Monaco. A daylight battle meant police, investigations, the inevitable questioning. Publicity was poison, and the mobster shunned exposure as a night-feeding carnivore avoids the sun.

But now he was committed to the chase, without alternatives, forced to see it through, whatever the result. There was no turning back.

He had taken all precautions possible, he had mobilized an army for the job—and still the outcome was in doubt. A long block up ahead, the hare was running flat out with two carloads of gunners on his tail.

The Corsican's chauffeur was keeping them in sight, but cautiously, prepared to reinforce the troops only if the quarry turned to make a stand.

Genet, the Corsican's lieutenant, had provided them with rendezvous coordinates, the scheduled meeting place pinpointed by a Sûreté official on the payroll of the *Union Corse*. An ambush in the parking lot had been impractical, but still Louis had hoped for a discreet transference of the ransom. Everything sounded so simple in the planning stages. . . .

The Citroën's lead had narrowed, and the trailing gunners pressed their quarry, crowding him, attempting to provoke a rash mistake. The snaking caravan was clear of the casino district now, and running through a neighborhood of modest shops and homes. The set was not ideal, but if the strike force could overtake him here, they had a chance.

Louis picked up the walkie-talkie, brought it to his face, keyed the button for transmission. He was in communication with the spearhead at last, prepared to call the shots, and there was very little time to lose.

"Close in," he snapped. "Thomas, Henri, take him *now*!"

His driver goosed the Mercedes's accelerator, keeping pace, and in the seat behind him he could feel his own crew of gunners craning forward, hungry for a piece of the upcoming action. One of them drew back a submachine-gun bolt to bring up the round into his weapon's firing chamber.

And the Corsican could feel their tension and excitement. He matched it with his own. The predator remembered other kills; he missed the old exhilaration of the hunt, the thrill of mortal combat. A nagging apprehension, warning him of danger, was quickly smothered by the adrenaline of the moment.

Sharp, excited voices clamored at him from the radio receiver, static overriding noise as both teams tried to answer him at once. He cursed, held the transmitter button down, silenced all of them at once.

Intent upon the chase, he jabbed his elbow at the driver, urging him to greater speed.

Another moment now, another block until they overtook the Citroën and forced it to the curb with automatic weapons blazing. He slid a hand inside his jacket to free the Browning automatic from its shoulder rigging. He held the cannon in his lap. Ready.

The point car closed in.

And the Citroën cut hard right into a narrow side street. Its tires screamed, smoked on the pavement. The Peugeot overshot the intersection, drifting as the wheelman rammed the brake to the floor.

In second place, the Fiat's driver saw the

Citroën's maneuver in time to twist hard into the turn and career after the prey.

The Peugeot whined into hot reverse, fish-tailed, and nosed right around to join the chain of pursuit.

"Allez, allez," the mobster snapped. "Get after them!"

The driver grunted his acknowledgment and floored the crew wagon's gas pedal, milking five more screaming miles an hour out of her. Louis was trembling, and he gripped the armrest fiercely, knuckles whitened from the strain.

It was the killing time at last, and the Corsican was more than ready.

WITH LESS THAN ONE HUNDRED FEET to spare, Bolan floored the brake pedal, twisting hard on the wheel to put the Citroën through a screaming turn. The engine sputtered and nearly died, but he saved it at the last instant. The Citroën now faced toward the enemy.

There was only one way out, and the Executioner was taking it. He held the accelerator down, rear tires spinning, leaving smoking rubber on the pavement, then finding traction as the take off pushed him back against his seat. With the tiny Uzi in his left hand, he sighted out the window, lining up the shot as he closed the gap.

The enemy driver saw it coming, and he spun the wheel, veering away from Bolan's line of fire. Bolan corrected, squeezing off a short burst on the fly, and through the disintegrated windshield he saw the driver's face dissolve, becoming something less than human. He was past them in a heartbeat. Behind him the driverless Fiat began to drift, losing speed until a dead foot slipped off the clutch and the engine faltered and died.

Ahead of Bolan, the Peugeot's wheelman had seen it all go down. Thinking fast, he swung his car around broadside, blocking off the narrow street and penning Bolan in. Gunners were erupting from the car, seeking cover, weapons tracking onto target, but the driver kept his seat, ready to respond to any move Bolan made.

Bolan put the Citroën into a shuddering broadside skid. The Citroën crashed into the Peugeot, crumpling and shearing off the open starboard door, rocking the car on its springs.

Crouched behind the plug car, three gunners were knocked off balance by the stunning impact. Bolan swung the mini-Uzi up, sighting on the driver's pallid face. The guy had expected avoidance action from Bolan, not an all-out crash. In the suspended moment of changed expectations, Bolan stroked off a very short burst.

One second the guy was sitting there, mouth ovaled to emit a scream, and the next he was undergoing transformation—face exploding as his skull expanded to impossible dimensions, contents violently released.

The other guncocks recovered fast, coming to their feet behind the Peugeot, shouting in French. The language registered on Bolan the second before they opened fire—by then he was hunching over as a bullet whistled past his face.

He floored the accelerator, holding the wheel steady, feeling the vibration as his sedan grated down the Peugeot's length. With the small arms roaring at its mangled bodywork, his car broke free, showing them his tail and powering away with hellfire chewing up its ass.

Twenty yards out Bolan skidded to a halt, wanting to take out the bastards for good. He took the Uzi with him as he rolled out of the Citroën into a combat crouch. He saw the Fiat unloading three gunners.

Bolan was exposed. The hardguys were swinging their guns around. One of them was rapidly finding the range.

Bolan answered with the miniature Uzi, laying a wreath of steel-jackets around the burp-gunner's neck and blowing him away. Before the gunner's body hit the pavement,

Bolan's fire was tracking on. It scattered the other soldiers, dropping one of them and driving the other two for cover behind the Fiat. Bolan was probing for a hot spot and he found it as the Uzi emptied, the final rounds igniting fuel under the Fiat's hood. Another second and the hood blew off. A ball of oily fire rolled along the Fiat's length, consuming flesh and steel. A burning figure rolled away from the inferno, his strangled screams engulfed in flames.

Bolan reached lightning-swift inside the Citroën and came out with two extra clips for the Uzi. He reloaded, rising from his crouch to face the others when he saw a black Mercedes sliding to a stop beside the Peugeot, doors flying open, disgorging reinforcements.

There were close to a dozen guns against him now. One of the new arrivals was barking orders, manhandling hardguys into line. He was a scowling, bearlike man with slicked-back hair and heavy jowls, dressed in an expensive pearl gray suit. Bolan did not recognize the face, but he made the type at once.

The guy was a mobster, and Bolan knew instinctively that he was not sent by Paradine.

The Executioner braced himself to meet the charge. He was ready when they came for him, three gunners breaking out around the nose of the Peugeot, two more pounding into view around the tail of the Mercedes. They were firing as they came, and their comrades behind the car were laying down a covering barrage.

Bolan ducked below the leaden hail, rolling out to his right, toward the nose of the Citroën. Around him, the sedan was taking repeated hits. The three soldiers circling his left flank were thirty yards out when Bolan gained his chosen vantage point, leaping out to take them unaware.

Bolan had put his faith in speed, accuracy and the element of surprise.

It paid off.

The big guy caught them flat-footed with a blazing figure eight, the hot steel-jackets ripping in at chest level, sweeping them away. Two of the gunners fell together, sprawling on the pavement in a bloody, tangled heap, but their companion on the right was slower going down. He was kneeling in the street, still fumbling to get off a shot with mangled hands, and it took another burst to put him on his back.

That left the gunners who were providing cover, and the Executioner was moving to meet them as the cover fire converged on his position. Diving, rolling, he slithered back along the Citroën's length, Uzi probing out ahead. The tiny subgun made for almost limitless body maneuverability.

It was a worm's-eye view, and he saw the enemy from the knees down. There were two pairs of pumping ankles in his sights when he stroked the trigger and let the muzzle drift from left to right. Twenty yards downrange, the gunners stumbled, crying out in pain. One of them dropped his machine pistol. His side-kick was clinging to a stubby automatic, but getting nowhere with it as the impact left him breathless. Bolan did not give him time to catch his second wind. The Uzi chattered again, dispatching half a dozen parabellum manglers. Both gunners died on their bellies, groveling in blood and misery.

Bolan fed a fresh magazine into the Uzi's pistol grip. He was on his feet and moving out of cover when he saw his enemies mysteriously begin to die.

One of the gunners was near his boss when his skull exploded into bloody fragments. Bits and pieces of the guy were running down the boss's face, soaking through his flashy jacket, when a second hardman sprawled across the hood of the Mercedes, dark blood pumping from his mangled throat.

Only then did Bolan hear the firing, the heavy-metal thunder that rolled in from somewhere behind the enemy. Someone had joined the battle, squeezing off precision rounds from a heavy-caliber assault rifle.

Another guncock was spinning out of view, clutching at a shattered face with dying hands, when Bolan made his move. The first announcement of his sprinting approach was the deadly chatter of his weapon. Two of the remaining soldiers never even turned to face him; riddled where they stood, both were lifted off their feet and cast away like broken mannequins.

Bolan stitched a third distracted gunner from crotch to throat.

The leader was alone, and Bolan found him kneeling in the shadow of the black Mercedes. He was empty-handed.

Sirens sounded in the distance as Monegasque police responded to the blazing firefight.

The mobster was clearly no more anxious than Bolan for a confrontation with the gendarmes. With a snarl of fury, he flung himself at an automatic pistol on the tarmac nearby, big hands clutching at salvation that was hopelessly beyond his reach.

Bolan let the Uzi rip, firing damn near point-blank at the human target. Flesh and fabric rippled with the drumming impact.

There was no time to swap the bullet-punctured Citroën. He reached the battered vehicle on a dead run and fired the engine, relieved to hear it running smoothly. With any luck the car would see him safely to his next checkpoint.

If there were no more ambushes along the way.

And if the scarred Citroën did not attract police.

Someone had helped him, and there was that to think about as he put the car in motion, powering away. Two wheels jounced across the curb as he passed the Mercedes, the Citroën growling toward the open road. Emergency lights were winking at him from the rearview mirror as he gave the Citroën its head, racing down the first major side street and running free toward the next rendezvous with Paradine's ambassador of death.

Toward Chiasso.

8

SARAH SHEPHERD STRETCHED PAINFULLY, trying to make herself comfortable on the concrete floor. Her legs and back were stiff, her shoulders sore from resting against the corrugated-metal wall behind her.

She was huddled in a corner of a Quonset hut that housed the diplomatic hostages, who were under constant guard by half a dozen terrorists, each carrying an automatic rifle slung across his shoulder. Any sudden movement by the prisoners, any conversation louder than a whisper, and an angry warning spewed from the nearest sentry.

The hut, about forty feet long, was one of several structures tightly grouped inside a barbed-wire fence. The terror-site reminded Sarah of an abandoned military post. Their prison was apparently a former barracks with the bunks and other furnishings removed. At one end, behind another corrugated wall, was a restroom and shower area. Their captors had removed the door from its hinges, and the open doorway was guarded constantly by a stern, silent rifleman.

She had seen the blond terrorist only briefly during the day, but Sarah knew he was the leader. She had watched him as he issued tight-lipped orders to the riflemen, addressing them in fluent German, Italian, and a language that sounded to her like Arabic. When he spoke, they listened and obeyed without question.

Thoughts of him reminded Sarah of the 747's jarring, hair-raising landing on a straight stretch of lonely rural highway, her own terror as the aircraft wallowed to a grinding halt that sheared off the landing gear. Terrorist reinforcements had been waiting for them on the ground.

From the makeshift landing strip, they were driven more than thirty winding miles in canvas-covered military trucks until they reached the isolated compound.

The terrorists were a motley crew—the spearhead of Americans who came aboard the plane disguised as federal agents and a larger force of Germans, Palestinians and Italians. As a group, they were having trouble with communications, but the blond man dominated and organized them with his linguistic skill and sheer commanding presence.

He frightened Sarah more than all the

others put together. She did not know his
plan, beyond its obvious connection with the
conference, but she sensed that he would do
anything to achieve his aims.

The guards had finished changing shifts an
hour earlier, and one of the replacements, a
swarthy Palestinian, was staring fixedly at
Sarah from across the room. He seemed to be
debating something with himself, frowning
and shifting restlessly as he tried to arrive at
some decision. Sarah felt his eyes upon her;
he made her flesh crawl.

Finally, the decision made, he cast a furtive
glance to either side and crossed the room. He
stood in front of her, but she did not look
up at him until he spoke to her directly, a
single harsh monosyllable demanding her attention.

Sarah glanced up, her eyes met his, and she
shook her head to indicate a lack of under-
standing. He gestured with the autorifle,
motioning for her to rise, repeating the command.

Sarah felt a cold knot of fear growing in
the pit of her stomach, and she hesitated.
Desperation joined the fear inside her.

Impatiently, the gunman nudged her with
a booted foot. Sarah rose stiffly, stood in
front of him and forced herself to return his
gaze, unflinching. She felt the color rise in

her cheeks as he examined her from head to toe.

Apparently satisfied, he growled something unintelligible, and jerked his head in the direction of the open bathroom door.

Sarah stood still. The hardguy reached out and seized her by the arm. She tried to pull away, but his grip tightened, fingers digging deep into her flesh, the muzzle of his weapon jabbing into her side. Feeling numb, she let herself be led until they reached the restroom entrance.

Something turned over in her stomach and she fought to free herself from the tight restraining grip. Twisting in his grasp, she hit the Arab with her fist, striking a glancing blow against his stubbled cheek.

He shoved her through the entryway with enough force to make her stumble. Recovering, she spun to face her enemy, bringing up her hands, her fingers curling into sharp defensive claws.

The gunman kept one hand on the pistol grip of his assault rifle as he reached for her with the other. Sarah backed away from him, colliding with a metal sink. He was on her before she had a chance to duck aside. His stale breath was nauseating, and his clutching hand closed painfully around her breast.

She lashed out, fingernails raking jagged furrows down his cheek as she wrenched away from him. Part of her blouse came away in his hand.

The Arab snarled in pain, dabbing at his wounded face, withdrawing bloody fingers. He attacked, striking with such speed that Sarah never really saw it coming. Pain exploded in her skull and the next instant she was lying at his feet, deafened by the ringing in her ears.

She was dimly conscious of an uproar in the Quonset; she recognized the voice of her superior, the undersecretary, and then the terrorist was kicking her methodically, the heavy boot drumming into ribs and legs, pummeling her against the corrugated-metal wall. The salty taste of blood was in her mouth, and she was drifting on a cloud of pain.

Hopelessly, she began to scream.

PARADINE WAS ANGRY. The news out of Monte Carlo was disturbing and confusing. If his snipers had not intervened in time, the ambush might have been disastrous. And he would not let anything deprive him of his prize when he had come so far, risked so much.

He was pacing through the open courtyard

of his compound, checking on his men. They were tough, professional, but there was tension in the ranks and it was his task to keep things operating smoothly. Later, when the mission was completed, they could disband and butcher one another as they pleased, but the project, his vengeance, took priority.

The compound was perfect for his purposes—removed from local villages, adjacent to friendly Russian satellites, convenient for a swift retreat if necessary. It had been a base for Allied occupation troops in northern Italy.

In a pinch, the compound was defensible, but Paradine did not plan to make his stand there. He intended to emerge victorious, let revenge expunge the months of pain and humiliation he had suffered at the hands of Phoenix.

Paradine's eyes hardened at the thought of his enemy, their first encounter and his brush with death.

Paradine despised Phoenix for making him afraid. He had learned the fear of death and failure when they had clashed in Turkey, and fear had walked beside him ever since. For the first time, Paradine had suffered doubts about his own ability, his mastery of the world. And he had learned to live with nightmares. . . .

Only blood would wash the fear away, make him strong and whole again. Phoenix was the center of his universe, Paradine's obsession, and the mercenary knew he could never rest until the dark warrior's blood was on his hands.

He saw Phoenix frequently, in a recurring dream that haunted him since Turkey. In the dream, he saw a soldier dressed in black, battle-clad with weapons, approaching through the acrid smoke of battle. The face was indistinct, but the eyes were piercing, cold as death and filled with infinite contempt. Paradine was kneeling unarmed, all alone, deserted by his men and stranded in the awesome warrior's path. He cringed, cowering as the man drew near. But the man passed by him. As he saw the enemy retreating into misty darkness, Paradine was overcome with sweet relief—until he realized that he had soiled himself.

Even now, memory of the dream brought a sheen of perspiration to his forehead.

Soon he would have the vengeance that he needed to exorcise the nightmare forever. Very soon.

It had been difficult to trace Phoenix, even to the bare extent that Paradine had managed. There had been no solid trace of him in Turkey, but Paradine had friends and associates around the world, denizens of the dark underground where death and information are the prime commodities of trade. He picked up a rumor of the name Phoenix without initially grasping its importance. Only time and circumstance had brought the message home.

A Western agent of extraordinary capabilities had been reported active for several months, moving through the underground at will and leaving ruin in his wake. The man was everywhere and nowhere, a phantom drifting in and out of focus, choosing targets and eradicating them with surgical precision.

Rumor placed the agent in the Sông Hong delta, Vietnam, when a key POW had been liberated, and his name was whispered by survivors in the smoking ruins of a military installation at Aujila, Libya. Phoenix had infiltrated renegade Luke Harker's "war college" in Algiers, turning the training session into bloody chaos. The warrior had executed Ricardo "Rikki the Hyena" Roybal in the bargain, thereby eliminating Paradine's chief competition in the terrorist marketplace. There had been a lethal clash in California with the Asian, Nguyen Van Minh, and an agent matching Phoenix's description had unearthed the Russian mole, Karpetyan.

The German Zwilling Horde, a splinter of the Baader-Meinhof gang, had also met the shadow warrior, to their sorrow. Sibling founders of the Horde, the Morganslichts, were numbered in the final body count, and while Paradine had never cared for Thomas, he would miss Thomas's twin sister, Tanya, who had a knack for mixing sex and revolution.

Phoenix had even been associated with the elimination of the Russian troika that included the Hispanic, Munoz, and the Japanese, Yoshida, in that dark dawn in Cuba only weeks ago.

Phoenix had killed them all, and more; Paradine was certain of it. Save for luck, an accident of fate, he would have been among them, resting with the fallen. The angry scar beneath his gun arm was a brand, reminding him of debts outstanding.

The Phoenix code name did not tell him much, but Paradine had put enough together to surmise a nationality. His enemy was American, perhaps CIA or Army Intelligence; it did not really matter. He was linked with fiercely successful death squads and foreign legions, but essentially he stood alone.

No further knowledge had been necessary for his operation; once Paradine put the plan in motion, either Phoenix would respond, or he would not. From his sparse knowledge of the man, Paradine could not believe his foe would pass up the challenge.

Striding past the Quonset hut that housed his prisoners, he was distracted by the sound of screaming. The terrorist leader veered off course. Brushing past a pair of nervous-looking sentries, he entered the hut.

The screaming had subsided to a muffled sobbing, barely audible beyond the open bathroom door. Paradine could hear a male voice, recognizable at once, cursing fluently in Arabic, berating someone who did not or could not answer back. He strode past the guarded hostages and through the far door to find Ahmad standing tall above the youngest woman hostage, alternately cursing and kicking her.

A glance told the story—the woman's shredded blouse, a breast exposed, bloody tracks along the Arab's cheek. Paradine's eyes turned to ice behind the mirrored aviator glasses.

His voice cut through the hut.

"Enough!"

The Arab froze, one foot raised, set to land another blow. When he faced Paradine, the narrow eyes were frightened, searching for an exit. He licked dry lips, his pink lizard's tongue darting out and back, and he shifted the Kalashnikov assault rifle in his grasp.

Ahmad was trying to explain, words spilling out in rapid fire, but Paradine was not listening. The leader put on a practiced smile and kept it casual as he closed the gap, never looking at the woman on the floor. He could see the Palestinian relaxing, standing easy, trying to return the smile.

Without warning, Paradine was on him, reaching out to pluck the AK-47 from his hands. In the same fluid motion he reversed the weapon, whipped it up and over, left to right, wooden stock impacting on the Arab's jaw with a brutal crack. Ahmad fell writhing on the concrete floor, bloody spittle drooling from the mouth he could no longer close.

Paradine propped the rifle against a sink and swiftly reached down to seize the Arab by the collar of his khaki shirt, hauling the wiry gunner to his feet, holding him erect. For an instant they were eye-to-eye, and then Paradine drove the stiffened fingers of his right hand up beneath the Arab's breastbone, crushing the man's diaphragm and emptying the wind out of him.

Ahmad doubled over, retching blood, knees buckling. Paradine hit him with a vicious roundhouse kick, the heel of his paratrooper's boot connecting with the Arab's shattered jaw, hurling him sideways. The man collided head-on with a urinal and tumbled back, collapsing on the floor.

The terrorist was dying. Paradine stood over him and felt a mixture of accumulated anger and contempt welling up inside. Ahmad had broken discipline, and an example must be set for all the others. At the same time, Paradine could not deny the welcome animal exhilaration he derived from violent contact.

He began methodically to kick the fallen Arab, driving him across the bathroom floor, concentrating on the spine and kidneys. He felt the ribs give way, collapsing into vital organs. Ahmad quit groaning. His form was slack, unresponsive to the blows. The smell of urine, suddenly released, was heavy in the stagnant air.

Finally satisfied, Paradine retraced his steps, brushing past the woman on his way to the Quonset's front door. His men outside watched him in stony silence. They parted ranks at his approach. Paradine spoke to no one in particular.

"Clean up the mess," he snapped, waving toward the inside of the hut, and left them to the task of human waste disposal.

Paradine felt better, purged of anger for the moment. His treatment of the Palestinian had served a double function—it was educational, and it had been a warm-up for the main event, his confrontation with the man called Phoenix.

He was looking forward to it with grim anticipation.

9

BOLAN CROSSED THE BORDER south of Breil and entered Italy, holding a northeasterly course. He avoided major towns because of damage to the Citroën from his firefight, making up the time by speeding on country roads. As the soldier drove mechanically, his mind was busy with the convoluted puzzle that his mission had become.

First on Bolan's mind was the Monte Carlo firefight. He was convinced the ambushers were mobsters, bent on killing him and taking the ransom for themselves. If he was right, if the gunners had not been dispatched by Paradine, there was a leak somewhere... with the Americans, perhaps the Sûreté, even in the terrorist camp. Whichever, the implications for his mission were ominous.

If outside forces were aware of Paradine's demands, and of the American decision to respond and the route he was following, anything could happen on the road.

He was certain that the leak would not in-

clude specifics of his mission or identity.
Stony Man security was absolute, inviolate.
As for destination, Bolan left the Monte
Carlo battlefield without survivors, and he
hoped the problem had been taken care of.
Except. . . .

The second riddle clamored for attention,
crowding out the first. Some snipers had
helped him out back there, enabling him to
wipe out the mobsters. It was clear the snipers
knew Bolan's route and something of his mission, and that they wanted Bolan to proceed.
The gunners could be following him even
now, or waiting up ahead, setting yet another
trap at Paradine's convenience.

Bolan shrugged it off. He had known the
mission was a suck from the beginning, and
an extra complication would not put him off
the scent. He owed it to the hostages—and
to all the future victims who would suffer
if he failed to stop Paradine once and for
all.

He was seeking out the dragon's lair, carrying the purifying flame. This time, the Executioner would not give up until he had
destroyed the serpent.

Or until he died in the attempt.

Bolan never wasted time thinking about
death. He was too damned busy living, making every moment count for something posi-

tive, taking every opportunity to strike another blow against the enemy.

Judgment day would be a search for scars instead of medals, and the Executioner had plenty of scars on his body and his soul. There would undoubtedly be more before his course was run, but he would never bear the mark of inaction, the stain of having seen his duty clear and turned away.

A fighter from youth, Mack Bolan knew only one way to play the game of life. He played to win, and there could never be a substitute for victory against the savages.

He would keep the rendezvous with Paradine's emissary at Chiasso, facing any other challenge he encountered on the way. It was his destiny.

APRIL ROSE HELD THE LASER WAGON at a steady seventy miles per hour along the coastal highway, keeping open water on her starboard flank. She ticked off the seaside towns— Cannes, Antibe, Cagnes-sur-Mer. Clearing Nice, she felt the tension building inside her. Bolan's rendezvous at Monaco was less than twenty miles away.

April knew Bolan had been right about the Laser Wagon. It was indeed conspicuous. But if they ran into an army they would need the extra firepower; the trick would be to follow him discreetly, making sure that neither Bolan nor the enemy discovered her along the way. Of the two, she was more concerned with Bolan sighting her, and she was grateful for the tracking system that would let her keep tabs on the Citroën at considerable distances.

If nothing happened. If he did not leave the car. . . .

April felt the chill of fear again, and she knew instinctively that there was something wrong with this assignment. Granted it was a trap, with Bolan walking into it prepared, but there were still countless risks that he could not foresee, infinite possibilities for betrayal and ambush. Several nations were involved, and April knew that any leak, anywhere along the line, could jeopardize Bolan's life and risk exposure of the whole Phoenix program.

For the first time since she met Mack Bolan, April was running the risk of disobeying him. Under other circumstances, such defiance would have been unthinkable. But right now she was reasoning with head and heart together as one, and she sensed that the soldier needed reinforcements.

There was no way she would let him run the gauntlet by himself. No way.

She entered Monto Carlo from the west,

duplicating Bolan's route as far as the casino, searching for a turnoff from the curving boulevard of the mountain-hugging coastal town that would take her down to the marina. Time was of the essence if April was to overtake him inside the city limits of this spectacular resort.

April keyed a video display on the pilot console, punching up a miniature projection of the city's winding streets, checking her position in relation to the harbor. The Laser Wagon's on-board computer banks contained identical intelligence on every European capital, and perhaps a hundred major cities in the United States and Canada. It was a vast, sophisticated road atlas, ever ready at the pilot's fingertips.

April found her position and was preparing for a turnoff at the next major cross street when she heard the sound of sirens closing on her flank. A speeding convoy of police cruisers passed her on the left, lights flashing, sirens drowning out the other sounds of traffic. Something did a slow barrel roll inside of April, and she sensed that she should follow.

It was a hunch, but she had learned from Bolan to respect gut instincts.

She slipped in behind the speeding squad cars, hanging back a block or two. The lights and sirens simplified her job, helping her keep the other cars in sight without attracting undue attention to herself.

They were leading her away from downtown Monte Carlo, leaving the casino and the harbor behind. If her hunch was wrong, she would lose any chance of picking up Bolan inside the city, but she toughed it out, staying with the hounds.

And she was with them when they slowed, cutting a hard right into a narrow side street that opened up between attractive shops. Other officers were already on the scene, deployed to traffic duty, trying to untangle the inevitable snarl of gawkers.

As she rode the brake, creeping toward the intersection, April saw an ambulance emerging from the side street, running with its lights and siren off. As it passed her going south, she caught a glimpse through the side windows of bloody bundles in the back.

April made the intersection, rubbernecking like a tourist, taking in as much as possible before the gendarmes waved her on. Uniformed police and plainclothes detectives sifted around the scene, taking notes and picking up the pieces from the urban battlefield.

Two cars—a black Mercedes and a small sedan—were parked together near the corner, and the smoking ruin of a third machine was visible inside the cul-de-sac.

Cameramen were snapping photographs of everything, and white-frocked attendants from a second ambulance were busy bagging bodies.

April did a double-take, searching for the Citroën. It was nowhere in sight, and she nearly choked on the sudden rush of relief.

Her soldier was gone, but he had been there, and recently. April Rose was certain of it. A Bolan hit was unmistakable.

Whatever else the carnage in the cul-de-sac might indicate, she knew that Bolan was continuing his mission, driving toward his rendezvous with Paradine. Nothing short of death would hold him back.

A traffic officer was motioning her on, and April waved back at him, rolling the almost-black battle wagon across the intersection, heading north. Her mind was working overtime, crowded with a rush of vital questions jostling for priority. She wondered who had tried to intercept the ransom, whether Paradine could be involved. If he was not, how had John Phoenix's mission been exposed?

Was Mack safe?

April knew the answer. Even if he left the battlefield unscathed, he was anything but safe as long as Paradine survived—he was merely passing out of danger and into even greater peril. There was nothing April Rose could do to stop him.

But there might be something she could do to help him.

She concentrated on the sensitive receiver of the battle cruiser's tracking system, with the video display of Monte Carlo and environs still visible. If the Citroën was anywhere within three miles, she would be able to detect him and plot his course.

A slight delay and then she had him, a blip running north and east along a road away from Monte Carlo. His present course would take him through the mountains into Italy—and somewhere beyond the border he would find a spider waiting in the center of its lethal web.

April meant to be there when he made the final confrontation.

She would stand with him, and fall beside him if it came to that.

April Rose would not have it any other way.

10

IN ITALY HE HAD BEEN KNOWN as *Il Bòia*, a rough translation of The Executioner, and Mack Bolan felt a sense of anticipation as he began his third visit to the troubled nation. He steered the Citroën north through hilly Lombardy, climbing steadily, leaving the foothills of the northern Apennines behind. Bolan was revisiting a land that had already presented him with two battlefields.

His reputation had preceded him the first time, putting Old World mafiosi on alert to stop the blitzing bastard who was slaughtering their brothers in America. They were waiting for him, but they were far from ready. It was Bolan's task to teach them a bloody lesson in proper preparation.

A new invasion of America was being planned when the Executioner arrived. Trained *gradigghia*, the seasoned killers also known as *malacarni*, were being shipped as reinforcements for the dwindling stateside ranks.

Italy, her soil steeped in seven centuries of gang-related bloodshed, was home for the Honored Society. When the Executioner arrived in Naples to confront the Boss of Bosses, *Don* Tronfio Frode, more blood had been spilled as he blitzed the city and left the Frode family in smoking ruins. But Bolan's primary target had been elsewhere, to the south, in Sicily's Agrigento province. There, at Naro, he had written the end to *Don* Cafu's *Scuola Assassino*, the assassins' school that was flooding North America with Mafia reinforcements.

On his second visit to Italian soil, the Executioner had come as the reborn Colonel John Macklin Phoenix. Bolan and his ally, Leo Turrin, met with terror in Tuscany, and once again Bolan applied the cleansing flame of righteous anger.

Now he was back, risking it all again. Bolan was not looking for the Mafia or any other local savages this time—but he would take them when and where he found them. If the Brotherhood tried to interfere with his mission, he would gladly tear through them on his way to Paradine.

It would be the Mafia's misfortune.

The American warrior reached Chiasso on schedule. He circled the outskirts of the picturesque border town, sizing up the place before he sought his checkpoint on the central square. By the time he arrived at the square, the Executioner had marked his exit points, each prioritized for suitability in different emergencies.

Chiasso is not a tourist town, despite the beauty of its alpine surroundings, and foot traffic on the square was light, without the fevered crush of Monaco. People moved with purpose and deliberation.

An ornate hotel, decorated as a Swiss chalet, was the village centerpiece. Other buildings on the square were shops surmounted by living quarters on the second story. Bolan felt the curious villagers watching him discreetly, checking out the stranger and his bullet-punctured vehicle. If there was a constable in town, he would quickly be apprised of Bolan's arrival. The warrior knew that time was short; he could not explain the Citroën's condition, and he did not intend to try.

Bolan circled the square twice before he spotted Paradine's ambassador. Emerging from the hotel lobby, the man was waiting for Bolan. He looked out of place in a business suit. He acknowledged Bolan with the bare suggestion of a nod, and began to follow the Citroën along the block until they reached a side street. Bolan found a parking space and waited by the car as his contact approached.

A muscular physique and holstered weaponry were evident beneath the gunner's business suit.

"Welcome to Chiasso, Mr. Phoenix. You have something for the People's Army." Bolan noted the German-accented English.

"I have something for the chief," the Executioner corrected him. "Delivery is strictly one-on-one."

The German guncock scowled at him, narrow lips compressed into a slit.

"I have orders to inspect the merchandise and verify its authenticity."

Bolan recognized the logic. He knew that if he balked, he would abort the mission and doom the hostages to certain death.

"I'd like a little privacy," he answered, glancing up and down the narrow street.

"I have rooms at the hotel," said the contact. "You are armed?"

The guy knew the answer, and Bolan did not even try to bluff it out. He gave the terrorist a narrow smile.

"Relax," Bolan said. "I'm not here to hold you up."

His contact frowned, plainly uncomfortable with the thought of taking on an armed opponent.

"Come," he said at last, and started off in the direction of the square.

Bolan got his satchel from the Citroën's trunk, then fell in step behind the terrorist. As he walked, the warrior kept his free hand inside the open flap of his coat, fingers locked around the mini-Uzi submachine gun at his waist. His jacket was primed with grenades, hidden at stomach height in the lining, available by reaching into slits.

THE WAITING HAD BEGUN TO TELL on Giovanni Goro. Essentially a man of action, he had never taken well to stakeouts. If there had been a choice, he would have opted for a hit-and-run guerrilla war, his force forever on the move from one encounter to another.

But idleness and waiting were the necessary evils of an urban terrorist's existence. Opportunities did not present themselves with clock-work regularity, and hardmen in the field spent more time hiding, lurking in the shadows, than they ever did in combat. Sometimes, Goro felt that boredom was a greater peril than the able gunmen of the GIS. Each year, he lost a score of soldiers to defection, seeking other outlets for their revolutionary rage; and others lost it all, breaking beneath the strain, and sacrificed themselves in suicidal violence.

Anything to end the waiting.

Sometimes, however, the prize was worth it. Today was such a time. The hijack ransom payment, once they liberated it from the delivery boy, would put the failing Red Brigades in fighting trim. Indeed, they might at last secure financial independence from the Mafia, finally wash their hands of petty crime and kidnapping for ransom.

Giovanni Goro did not see himself as having anything in common with the standard criminal. The hoodlum, be he mafioso or the lowest sneak thief on the street, was a parasite, drew nourishment from working men the way a leach devours blood from healthy animals. The Red Brigades, in contrast, were political fighters. They were artists of terror. They were merchants who dealt in the commodity of ideology—the taking of the human mind, and, regrettably but necessarily, the taking of human life.

If the revolutionaries sometimes imitated mafiosi in their tactics, even joined the Honored Brotherhood for special projects, it was all a matter of expediency. In time, when they achieved their victory, the gangster allies would be swept away with all the other vermin—priests and private businessmen, the capitalists and fascists who were guardians of the hated status quo.

A change was coming, yes, and taking longer than the Red Brigades had first believed. The people, ignorant of politics in general and revolution in particular, were squeamish still about the necessary tactics Goro and his troops employed—but they would come around in time.

A healthy cash reserve would fill the army's ranks and arsenals, speed up the schedule of their revolution. Soon, perhaps within the hour, Giovanni Goro would have everything he needed to ensure a victory.

Across the street, his secondary target was returning with the courier in tow. Giovanni marked the German—face remembered from a former failed alliance with the Baader-Meinhof gang—and automatically dismissed him, concentrating on his tall companion. At a glance, he knew the waiting was about to end.

The new arrival was a tall man, broad across the chest and shoulders. Goro could read nothing in his face—neither fear nor any vestigil excitement—and the stranger seemed at ease, as if he had prepared himself for anything and knew that he could cope with it when it arrived. His open coat might easily conceal a weapon.

But it was the satchel in his hand that riveted the terrorist's attention. Black and obviously heavy, though the big man carried it without apparent effort, it contained the secret of Goro's future. Giovanni and his troops had traveled from Milan at great risk to life and liberty, had staked out the old hotel for hours, all with the aim of picking off this courier, and relieving him of his valise for once and all.

They would succeed today, or they would die in the attempt. Goro was committed beyond all choice. If they failed, there could be no retreat. There would be nowhere to retreat to.

He watched the German and his new companion reach the hotel's double doors and disappear inside. Another hostile soldier watched the lobby; he had been sitting there since early afternoon when Giovanni crossed the narrow street and went inside to check it out, pretending he was lost and looking for a nonexistent tenant.

That made three guns inside, another two in back of the hotel. The hijackers were covering themselves, but they were counting on victim cooperation, never thinking that an outside force might try to intervene.

It was a small mistake, as fatal ones so often are.

Giovanni Goro turned from the second-story window, nodded to the clutch of gunners waiting by the door.

"We go."

Passing by the folding card table, he retrieved his squat Beretta submachine gun, racked the bolt back and eased the safety off. Another moment, two or three at most, and all the waiting would be over. He could taste the new excitement, feel it mounting in him as they reached the stairs and started down. A hard, unfeeling smile was etched across his face.

He smelled the victory, could feel it just within his grasp. The ransom was as good as his, but taking it away would be half the pleasure.

BOLAN'S CONTACT LED HIM through the hotel lobby. As they entered, Bolan saw a second hardman seated by the door.

Up one flight of stairs, Bolan and the guide reached a narrow corridor, rooms off either side. A lookout was waiting for them in the hallway, his wooden chair kicked back against the wall, hard eyes tracking Bolan's every move. The German opened a door and led the way inside. Bolan found himself inside a comfortable suite. He noted double windows opposite the door, offering a view of the alley below.

Bolan left his satchel on the coffee table and chose a chair that let him watch both the door and window. He was not expecting trouble from the German, but the Monte Carlo suck had shown him the degree to which danger lay on every side.

His contact opened the satchel. Cautious, hesitant, he stirred the diamonds with a finger, quickly estimating numbers. He selected three diamonds, lined them up in front of him and fished a jeweler's loupe from an inside jacket pocket. Bolan watched him as he picked up the first stone and held it up against the light for scrutiny.

The German seemed to know his business. He examined the stones professionally, verifying authenticity and quality. Finally satisfied, he dropped them back inside the satchel, closed it and pocketed the loupe.

"Very well," he said. "You may proceed with the delivery as planned."

"Where and when?"

"Your final checkpoint is at Udine, near the Yugoslav border. You'll be met at the Café Vittorio and given your directions to the drop."

"Time?"

The German checked his watch, calculating.

"Three hundred fifty kilometers. You should be at the café by six o'clock. Enjoy your supper."

Bolan gave the terrorist an icy smile. He was on his feet and reaching for the satchel when he heard the sound of muffled gunfire. Somewhere on the floor below, a pistol opened up, automatic weapons quickly joining in and drowning out the first reports. A rising scream was smothered by the rapid-fire explosions.

The German terrorist was rising, groping for his holstered weapon, but the Uzi got there first. Nosing through the open flap of Bolan's overcoat, muzzle inches from the gunner's face, it commanded complete attention.

"One second, one chance," Bolan snapped. "What's going down?"

There was confusion mingled with terror on his captive's face, and the German spread his hands in a helpless gesture.

"A trap. I don't know...."

Pounding footsteps reached the landing and moved along the corridor. Outside, the sentry in the hallway raised a warning cry and automatic weapons answered, bullets smacking into flesh and plaster. Something heavy struck the door and rebounded with a crash.

Bolan heard voices arguing in rapid-fire Italian. The doorknob jiggled, and a boot heel slammed ineffectually against the solid door.

Then weapons thundered in the hall, bullets eating up the wood and latch mechanism.

The German terrorist rushed past Bolan in a flash, sprinting for the window and freedom. Bolan, helping him along with a short burst between the shoulder blades, saw the hardguy sail on a hard collision course—he hit the window squarely and burst through, taking glass and sash bars with him in his headlong plunge.

Bolan pivoted and held the mini-Uzi's trigger down, tracking across the room from left to right. Steel-jackets drilled through the lathe-and-plaster wall and cut a ragged figure eight across the door. Another body hit the boards outside, and the hostile fire momentarily faltered.

Bolan grabbed his satchel from the coffee table and stitched another line of holes across the door as he backpedaled toward the window. Swinging the satchel, he cleared some shards of glass and clambered through. He saw the platform of a fire escape immediately below him.

Bolan high-stepped over the dead thug, heading for the metal stairs. His foot was on the top rung when bullets chipped masonry above his head.

His enemies had the back door covered.

Bolan spotted two bastards crouched behind a large trash bin below. Both wore ski masks and olive-drab fatigue jackets.

Autoloading pistols were finding the range.

Bolan drove them under cover with a long burst and used the breathing room to fish a thermite grenade out of an inside pocket. He yanked the pin and made his pitch, dropping the deadly egg directly in the trash bin.

It detonated with a hollow roar, the shock wave knocking both gunners off their feet. Chemicals and garbage combined in a fiery mushroom, superheated comets streaking off in all directions, raining down around the Executioner on his perch.

Bolan skipped the stairs and vaulted high across the railing of the fire escape. He saw the plug men busy fighting for their lives, beating at the flames with burning hands. He took them out with a single burst that silenced screaming, ended pain.

The trap was closing fast, with Bolan at its center. Overhead, gunfire erupted on the fire escape. Bullets whispered around him. One 9mm round hit his satchel and spent most of its force among the precious stones.

Bolan sent a burst in that direction, saw a hooded sniper stumble, lurch across the railing and sail into free-fall.

Fifty yards of open pavement lay between the soldiers and Bolan's wheels. He was surrounded by a force of undetermined origin and numbers, on a killing ground selected by the enemy. Given the circumstances, there was only one way to go.

He would continue on the offensive, carrying the fire. All the way to hell or victory.

11

Bolan fed his mini-gun another magazine as he approached the mouth of the alley. He was running hell-bent when a lone terrorist leaped in front of him, brandishing a Mauser automatic. Bolan smashed him in the face with his satchel. The hard canvas, weighted with precious stones, knocked the guy to the pavement with all the force of Bolan's explosive advance. The big guy pinned the terrorist with a precision burst through the chest.

Troops were spilling out of the hotel and swinging anxious weapons toward Bolan. The Executioner scattered them with parabellum sweepers, dropping two and driving back the rest. Then he was in motion, dodging, weaving like a quarterback under attack. Other guns had opened up across the street, bullets knocking chips of stone and plaster off the wall behind him. Bolan answered, firing blind, keeping both eyes on the corner that could make or break him.

And then he saw the enemy sedan across

the street. The driver spotted him and began revving. He came off the mark with smoking tires. Half a dozen guns were blasting at Bolan from the car. He hit the pavement in a bruising headlong dive, the holstered 93-R digging hard and deep into his ribs, the satchel slapping the ground. He cut the mini-Uzi in a sweeping arc, locking onto target as the gap was closed. He stroked the trigger and saw the driver's startled, torn face. Dying hands were frozen on the steering wheel, deadweight dragging hard to starboard. Suddenly the dark sedan skidded broadside, going over in a roll. A door sprang open to expel one dead terrorist, and Bolan heard the other gunners cursing, screaming.

Bolan was up and running as the stricken vehicle came to rest against a lamp post. There were enough guns against him; he could not spare the numbers necessary for a mop-up.

Bolan made the corner under fire, and a rifle bullet traced across his thigh, almost knocking him off stride. He could see the Citroën; it was within his reach, and he put on a desperate burst of speed.

Shutters banged open on an upstairs window across the street, and Bolan knew he was in trouble before the light machine gun opened fire. Hidden gunners saw his destination, and they were firing at the vehicle, armor-piercing bullets slicing through the roof and doors, safety glass disintegrating into a thousand small cubes. One tire exploded, then another, as the Citroën shuddered under the lethal rain.

He was thirty feet from the vehicle when the gunners found their mark. The Citroën exploded, spewing fiery hell.

The concussion lifted Bolan off his feet and hurled him against the wall with stunning force. Searing waves of heat attacked him, stealing his breath. The shaken soldier tried to drag himself behind the smoky remains of his car.

APRIL ROSE APPROACHED CHIASSO from the south, slowing when she had the town in sight. She had followed Bolan to the little mountain town with grim, tenacious skill. Outside the larger cities, her computer atlas was restricted to an overview of major highways. North of Genoa and Milan she had to navigate by feel—aided by the tracking system's sensitive direction finder. She could plot the Citroën's coordinates, determine intervening distance, but she could still overshoot the mark and lose precious time if Bolan had deviated from the main route.

Chiasso was another problem. Despite its

size, a street-by-street reconnaissance was risky, time-consuming. There were places where a car and a man could disappear without a trace, and April knew she could lose her soldier.

The place to start was downtown, a centralized location that would get her a fix on Bolan's general direction. Once she had obtained a compass point and defined the target area, April could begin a systematic search of streets and alleys. She would have to swallow her impatience, take the time to do it right.

She was closing in on the heart of town, and the Laser Wagon's tracking system was responding. Greater strength and frequency of audio-response signals told her that the Citroën was close and that she was drawing nearer; the video display revealed it as a blip at center screen.

April turned the corner and found the Citroën parked against the curb a hundred yards ahead of her. She felt a rush of mingled apprehension and relief. She drove by the empty car looking for Striker, or at least a sign, a clue, of where he was.

April continued past the Citroën and turned onto the square. There she found a welcoming party.

Half a dozen troops in matching O.D. jackets clustered at the entrance of a small hotel, an equal number grouped across the street on lookout duty.

Hard-eyed faces turned to watch her through the windows of a black sedan, parked against the curb with engine idling. A rifle barrel protruded above the windowsill.

April counted twenty guns around the square. She saw no sign of Bolan.

He could be in the hotel, or any other building on the piazza. If he was aware of danger, he would bide his time, select the moment and the place to strike. All she could do was make herself available to help.

April drove along the square, feeling hostile eyes tracking her all the way. She turned left at the intersection, fighting down an urge to run, easing off the gas until the troops were out of sight. When several blocks of houses lay between them, April let the battlewagon loose, accelerating back along a route parallel to the one she had just driven.

She felt tension building up explosively inside her, knuckles whitened as she tightly gripped the steering wheel.

She was two blocks away from the square when she heard the first reports of gunfire, muffled but distinct, the popping of a handgun, the crackling counterpoint of automatic weapons. The battle had begun.

She stood on the accelerator. The metallic

taste of fear was in her mouth. April swallowed it, allowing anger to enfold her and burn the fear away.

She was primed to kill for the man she loved. April Rose was coming to the hellgrounds.

BOLAN WAS SURROUNDED. Crouching, he tried to keep the smoking carcass of his car as a screen between himself and the second-story gunners. Bolan's face was cut and bleeding from the flying shards of steel and chips of concrete.

The street was filled with troops sniping at him, circling for position. A bullet grazed his shoulder. He wriggled closer to the fire and felt its fierce heat. Another moment, and the enemy would be ready for the rush.

Bolan could feel the noose around his neck, but there was no surrender in the warrior. Laying the satchel down beside him, he prepared for the fight of his life.

He heard them coming in a rush from both sides, boot heels clomping on the pavement, and he moved to greet them. He took on the right flank first, with a noisy parabellum daisy chain that cut the legs from under a determined trio and left them writhing in their vital juices on the sidewalk. Two rounds each to silence cries of agony, and then he spun around to face the danger at his back.

Two terrorists were closing on him from behind, pumping wild rounds in his direction. Bolan stroked the Uzi's trigger; the mini-weapon stuttered and emptied out a final dozen rounds along his backtrack.

It was sufficient. The lead gunner stumbled and dropped his automatic rifle as he took the brunt of Bolan's fire, choking on the contents of his ruptured lungs.

His companion, leaking from a line of holes across the lower abdomen, advanced a few steps before tumbling to the pavement.

Bolan yanked the Uzi's empty clip and replaced it with his last one. The rest, his whole supply of backup ordnance, had detonated with the Citroën. When the final magazine was spent . . . Bolan did not plan to be around.

He slipped the Beretta 93-R from its shoulder rig and double-checked the load. Fifteen rounds, plus the Uzi's thirty-two.

He scrambled to a fighting crouch behind the blackened Citroën, Uzi primed and ready in his right hand, Beretta in his left. His body was a coiled spring, ready to explode. His pulse throbbed in his ears and drowned out the roar of hostile guns.

Time to go.

The Executioner was rising from his crouch, braced and ready for flight, when a fiery comet streaked across his field of vision. It impacted on the window frame above the light-machine-gun nest and exploded in a ball of searing flame, devouring flesh. A pair of gunners on the street below were buried by an avalanche of shattered masonry.

A second fireball zeroed in on target and detonated in the intersection to his left. Bolan saw the clutch of startled soldiers scattering, vaporized before they had a chance to flee. Survivors on the flanks were busy looking for a place to hide.

He scanned along the rocket's track and saw the Laser Wagon. April Rose was already EVA and laying down a steady stream of automatic-rifle fire, toppling another pair of terrorists at fifty yards. Shaken troops were starting to recover, moving out to face the unexpected danger on their flank.

The Executioner had seen enough. He swung the Uzi up and squeezed the trigger. He held it down and swept the muzzle in a lethal arc across his field of fire. Parabellum shockers tore the straggled ranks apart and April joined the deadly chorus with her auto-rifle, turning the advancing enemy into a bloody rabble.

Firing at a cyclic rate of 600 rounds per minute, Bolan's mini-mangler spent its load in less than three seconds. He was moving, scooping up his satchel on the run, the Beretta probing out ahead of him for scattered targets. April covered his retreat with the assault rifle, backing toward the battlewagon while she held the hostile guns at bay.

She fired a parting burst along his track before she hopped back in the Laser Wagon. April had the big black motor home in motion by the time he found a seat beside her, standing on the gas and taking them away in a very nearly top-heavy swerve before the decimated foe could organize hot pursuit.

The soldier let himself relax in the powerful vehicle, willing knotted muscles to unwind. He ignored the pain of superficial wounds and concentrated on the woman next to him.

She had defied him, saved his life...and he would have to find a way to send her home again.

12

TWENTY MILES BEYOND CHIASSO, April found a turnout and roared the Laser Wagon in behind a stand of trees. She killed the engine and swiveled in the driver's seat to face Mack Bolan. Her smile was cautious, hesitant.

"You come here often, soldier?"

"Once is plenty. How about you?"

She faked a casual shrug.

"I was in the neighborhood, thought I'd drop by."

"You shouldn't be here, April."

"Hey, don't gush."

"Okay, what brings you to the front?"

"Just a hunch that you might need some help," she answered tartly.

"Does Hal know where you are?"

"More or less. He knows I'll be with you."

"*Were* with me," the Executioner corrected. "I still need to handle this alone."

"Like hell!" she snapped. "You ditched me once today, and that's your limit."

"You're getting in over your head."

April's anger seemed to melt away.

"Not a chance."

Bolan tried to frown but missed it by a hair.

"Dammit, April."

And then she seemed to see him for the first time, noticing the cuts about his face, dark blood seeping through the fabric of his slacks.

"You're hurt!"

"Nothing that a shower and some iodine won't fix," Bolan told her.

"Who's the doctor here?" she asked indignantly. "I want to check you over myself."

Bolan let her take his hand and lead him back along the battlewagon's central aisle, past computer banks and the armory to living quarters in the rear. There, he stripped off his clothes and battle rigging, and laid the tools of war aside. April moved around him, gentle fingers tracing recent wounds and ancient scars with equal tenderness.

April found the iodine and swabs and set about the task of cleaning his wounds. Bolan watched her work. The warrior's heart went out to her and he was glad, in spite of everything, to have her there.

She finished dabbing at the shallow leg wound and straightened up to meet his eyes.

"Is there. . . anything else I can do?"

Bolan smiled at the sudden color rising in her cheeks. He shook his head.

"Sorry. I've got a dinner date with Paradine at six o'clock."

But she was already moving, backing off a pace and sliding down the zipper of her jump suit, her bright eyes never leaving his.

"You have to take a shower anyway," she said. "We might as well save water."

Bolan watched her shed the outer skin, a graceful butterfly emerging. He could feel the warm response within himself, immediate, commanding. An affirmation of vitality in the face of violent death.

The warrior and the lady came together, joined, became as one. Neither sought a permanent escape; both were conscious of death's close proximity. They took the moment for themselves, made it last a loving lifetime. And for soldiers in an everlasting war, a moment had to be enough.

"HOW MANY MEN DID WE LOSE?" Paradine asked.

His lieutenant shifted nervously in his seat.

"All three at the hotel," he answered. "They never had a chance."

"Were any of them killed by Phoenix?"

"Hard to say. The place was like a shooting gallery."

Paradine stretched his legs beneath the army-surplus desk, rocking gently in his swivel chair. His mind was crowded with a rush of questions, and he felt confined, imprisoned in the small command hut. He longed to be pursuing Phoenix in the field, but he forced himself to concentrate on the immediate problem.

"Do we have a handle on the others?"

His lieutenant nodded.

"Several of the dead have been identified as Red Brigades."

Paradine cursed. For an instant he was blinded by anger. They had a leak, but there was nothing he could do about it.

"What about the woman?"

"Nothing solid," replied the lieutenant. "Phoenix didn't seem to be expecting her."

"But they left together?"

"That's the word. She was laying down some heavy fire to cover him."

"What are they driving?"

"Some kind of motor home. We shouldn't have any trouble spotting it if we decide to go ahead."

Paradine glanced up quickly.

"If?"

The lieutenant spread his hands.

"Phoenix violated your instructions. I assumed—"

"You assumed too much," Paradine interrupted him. "We're going on as scheduled."

"The woman?"

"She could be a problem," Paradine muttered. "If they're still together at Udine, I want her taken care of. Separate them, bring her back alive if possible. If not. . . ."

"Understood. And Phoenix?"

"No change. Send him on as planned. Either way it goes, he should be looking forward to the payoff."

"About our security. . . ."

"It doesn't matter now. Double up around the checkpoint. We can deal with internal problems later."

"Consider it done."

His aide hesitated at the door, turning to ask a parting question.

"Have you known about him for long? This Phoenix?"

The terrorist leader smiled, but his eyes were burning coals behind the silvered lenses.

"Forever," he replied.

Alone again, he tried to bring some order to the chaos of his thoughts. There were problems with security, that much was certain, and the intervention of outsiders threatened to snuff his plans.

Paradine stopped himself. There had been

no Red Brigades at Monte Carlo, and that meant two informers, or a single traitor selling information on the open market. Either way, he ran a risk of losing everything before the final payoff.

Phoenix could defend himself. He had proved it already.

He was good, but he was not invincible. It only took a single bullet, even accidentally fired, and the terrorist could be robbed of his revenge. The thought of losing Phoenix disgusted Paradine and left him nauseous, trembling with helpless fury.

He was not concerned that Phoenix was meeting opposition and being tested on the way, as long as he arrived with enough energy to make the climax interesting. Paradine was hungry for a chance to prove himself, for direct participation in the shadow warrior's death.

He put the thought away. Phoenix would arrive on schedule. Nothing would prevent him from accomplishing delivery of the ransom.

Nothing short of Paradine himself.

The mercenary realized that he had much in common with his enemy. Both were men of purpose, of exceptional ability and determined unto death.

Phoenix would survive his trials and make

the final rendezvous with Paradine because he had no choice. It was his destiny.

The terrorist removed his Browning auto-pistol from its holster and laid it on the desk top. Nimble fingers stripped the weapon down in seconds and began a ritual cleaning and testing of its working parts. The simple exercise allowed him to relax.

He thought about a bastard named Phoenix.

13

HEADING TOWARD THE FINAL CHECKPOINT, April took the Laser Wagon south then northeast, skirting the Alps on a path through fertile flatlands. Night was falling as they reached the outskirts of Udine, a town located twenty miles from the Yugoslav border.

The pair were in a very unsettled area. Italy had been experiencing trouble with her neighbors to the east—implications of Communist Bulgarian involvement with a wave of brutal kidnappings and an assassination attempt on the Pope. Udine's proximity to Yugoslavia had Bolan on alert to possible incursions by agents who had sponsored Paradine in previous acts of terrorism.

And he was not ruling out the possibility of KGB involvement in the mercenary's current hostage scheme. Personal revenge was certainly a motive, but the Soviets would stand to benefit from any action that destabilized the Middle East. The KGB field directors in

Belgrade would not hesitate to sacrifice a score of lives in the pursuit of influence and oil. They were on uncertain ground, and the Executioner would not relax his guard until all the players had been identified and dealt with.

April parked the battlewagon on a country lane outside of town and left the engine idling.

"I need a once-around before you drop me off," Bolan said. "Nice and easy, just to scope the neighborhood."

"That's a roger. I can spot a vantage point and cover you, in case there's trouble."

"Negative," he answered. "You're my lifeline. I want you out of sight and out of danger if it falls apart."

April's hurt and anger hung just beneath the surface.

"I thought we settled that," she said.

"We did."

"And I lost out?"

"We're not competing, April." Bolan let his voice soften. "If it sours, you're the ball game."

"Sure."

"Believe it."

Bolan saw the anger fade behind her eyes, replaced by sadness. The voice that answered him was distant.

"It isn't what I had in mind."

"Paradine is after me," he said. "I wouldn't want to disappoint him."

"I can help," she told him.

"And you have," he said. "You will again. But Paradine belongs to me."

He silenced April's protest with a gentle finger pressed against her lips. The lady met his gaze, saw his determination and slowly turned her eyes away. Without another word, she put the battlewagon into gear and took her soldier to a dinner date with Death.

URI NOSENKO CHECKED HIS WATCH and found he had another fifteen minutes to wait. Below his window, the street around the Café Vittorio was filled with people going home from work.

He was a patient man, used to waiting. He had learned that if he took the time to do a job right, he would be rewarded. It was true whether hunting animals or men. Besides, he enjoyed the hunt—the planning—even more than the kill.

Nosenko was a natural hunter. Circumstance had introduced him at an early age to the excitement of hunting game larger than fox or rabbit. As a teenager, he had crouched for twenty hours in the snow at Stalingrad waiting for a Nazi general to emerge from his command post. The episode had cost him several toes but earned him the Order of Lenin. His accomplishment was also noticed by an officer of some political ambition, and Nosenko's star began to rise.

There was work for patient killers in the postwar Soviet Republic, and Nosenko had risen through the ranks a pace or two behind his benefactor. When the Stalin purges came and dispatched his mentor to the Gulag and an early death, Uri showed patience and adaptability, shifting sides and moving onward, upward.

He had served Mother Russia for a generation, stalking enemies of the Republic in a dozen countries. Faces changed around the Kremlin, agencies discarded acronyms at will—the KGB and NKVD, SMERSH and GRU—but through it all the hunter persevered, practicing his craft with skill and equanimity. The identity of targets mattered little.

But targets mattered, obviously, to his masters. Illyanovich, for instance, had been excited when he called Nosenko in about the present job. He had tried to hide his nerves behind a casual facade, but Uri was adept at reading men. He knew before he took it that the mission was special. If he succeeded, there would be moments of reflected glory, with,

perhaps, some more substantial benefits. If
he should fail. . . .

Nosenko shrugged the thought away and
concentrated on his meager knowledge of the
target. Phoenix. Probably American, an extraordinary soldier even by Ivan's subdued
account. Uri had not heard of him before,
but that was no surprise. Agents often altered
names and faces.

Nosenko was uneasy on Italian soil. The
damned Bulgarians were ruining the area for
everyone—their foolishness with Pope John
Paul a prime example—but the hunter took it
as a challenge. Urgency demanded public execution; there was little hope of secrecy, but
with speed, efficiency, the friendly border
close at hand, Uri felt assured of success.

And he had turned the Café Vittorio into a
death trap. Located in the middle of the block
between a baker's shop and a tobacconist's,
the restaurant possessed a single entrance,
which he had covered thoroughly. His men
were on the rooftops opposite, waiting in cars
across the street, and mingled in with the flow
of sidewalk window-shoppers. Two of them
were dining in the restaurant, dawdling over
plates of pasta, waiting for the guest of honor
to arrive.

Phoenix was a dead man if he kept his date.
Others probably would die as well, but orders

from Illyanovich were long on urgency and short on caution. Elimination of the target had priority, and bystanders were expendable.

He checked the time again—five minutes left—and scanned the street to either side. There was nothing new or out of place, except—

A long, sleek motor home turned into traffic from a side street three blocks down. Nosenko watched it pass beneath him, slow and stately, a classy wagon complete with gold stripe and mysterious insignia. The insignia on its side was almost a provocation, almost a challenge—wings rising above flames.... The vehicle turned off again another two blocks east. Nosenko waited, but the pass was not repeated.

Alarms were sounding in the back of his mind.

He lifted the walkie-talkie, keyed the transmission button.

"Everyone alert," Nosenko snapped. "The target is approaching."

BOLAN LEFT APRIL, the diamonds and the Laser Wagon on a side street and approached his final checkpoint on foot from the west. His reconnaissance had not yet revealed a trap, but the warrior was vitally alert to danger as he moved along the streets.

Bolan again scanned the immediate area that housed the Café Vittorio. He registered at least a dozen high-potential sniper roosts before he gave up counting. If the enemy was waiting for him, he would know soon enough.

Outside the café, a dozen tables were arranged beneath a brightly colored awning. It was early for the dinner crowd; only two of the sidewalk tables were occupied. An aging couple was seated near the entrance, and at the far end of the patio a solitary man sipped wine and waited for his order. Bolan recognized his contact. He had seen the face before, in Monte Carlo.

Bolan took a seat and refused the guy's offer of a drink. A waiter appeared, hovering beside them, but was sent away.

"Is the package safe?"

"And ready for delivery," Bolan answered. "The hostages?"

"Are waiting for you, rather anxiously, I should imagine." The gunner looked him over carefully. "You've done well, Phoenix. My employer sends his compliments. The obstacles you met were...unexpected."

"Sloppy planning," Bolan said. "Somebody's got a security problem."

"We're looking into it. There should be no further interruptions."

"I'll need a time and place," Bolan said.

The terrorist watched him closely, searching for something behind his eyes. Instead of answering, the guy raised his glass and drained it in a single swallow.

Before Bolan heard the shot, he saw the wineglass explode in the contact's face, jagged splinters gouging cheeks and lips. The face collapsed into scarlet ruin. Teeth, bone, cartilage and a punctured eye were explosively released from their confinement as the victim's skull disintegrated.

Bolan was behind the table when the second bullet sliced the air above his head.

All around him, the scene had erupted in chaotic sound. Other weapons joined the hellfire chorus, pouring lead into the Café Vittorio, ignoring innocent pedestrians caught in the cross fire.

Screams from the wounded and dying mingled with the roar of guns.

14

BOLAN BRACED HIMSELF, legs bunched beneath him like steel springs. Then he flung himself headlong across the killground. A line of tumblers blazed inches from his face.

Bolan, mini-Uzi blazing, was prepared to risk it all and break on through the gunner lines when a pair of hardmen exploded from behind him.

The warrior turned and took them out with his one-handed submachine gun, ripping off a waist-high figure eight that disemboweled the guncocks where they stood. A single bullet, triggered by the nearest gunman as he died, hit the wall over Bolan's head and punched on through.

Tracking on, the Executioner triggered short, selective bursts in the direction of his scattering street-level targets. Only a few failed to reach cover, and they fell. It gave Bolan some breathing room.

A black sedan was rolling in along the curb, creeping at a snail's pace, weapons bristling from the window, joining in the fusillade. Bolan fired a random burst and heard bullets striking metal. He hid around a corner. Digging in a pocket of his coat, he pulled out a thermite grenade and jerked the pin. With a side-arm toss, the deadly metal sphere rolled across an open stretch of sidewalk. It dropped off the curb and disappeared beneath the enemy sedan.

The three-second fuse died, and with a hollow roar the vehicle became a rolling crematorium. A starboard door sprang open and a panicked figure leaped clear, spinning like a dervish on the curb before a rifle bullet dropped him into oblivion.

Moving under cover of the smoke and fire, Bolan wormed his way across this latest savage pasture, searching for an open field of fire. The enemy was closing on his flank. April and the Laser Wagon were a long run away. The Executioner would have to cut the odds, and quickly, if he hoped to leave the killing ground alive.

Survival took priority. Later he could worry about his severed link to Paradine and the rendezvous at an unknown place and time.

FROM HIS PERCH ABOVE the kill zone, Nosenko watched the ebb and flow of battle in amazement. Bodies littered both sides of the narrow street. Automatic fire riddled the picturesque facade of the Café Vittorio. Crouched behind a table near the open door, their solitary target was returning fire with deadly accuracy, sniping gunners as they showed themselves.

And a relatively simple execution had degenerated into total chaos while the Russian watched it happen. What he viewed from the window was enraging, almost paralyzing.

The target had surprised him, certainly, with both the speed and grim ferocity of his reaction. They were dealing with a soldier here, obviously an extraordinary one.

But Uri had the guns and numbers on his side. Defeat remained unthinkable. Defeat was beyond the realm of possibility.

Nosenko made a swift decision to commit the backup gunners. The clock was running, and authorities would be responding to the sounds of battle momentarily. His force had lost a quarter of its strength already, and the Russian could not risk a battle with police.

He raised the walkie-talkie, barked a curt command into the microphone. Below him, barely audible above the roar of gunfire, an engine growled to life, accelerating through the lower gears. Peripherally, he saw the black sedan as it moved from an alley into striking range, its complement of gunners craning for a clear view of their target.

Overhead, his rooftop snipers must have seen the backup car, for the volume of their enfilading fire redoubled, pinning down the soldier where he lay. The Russian smiled his pleasure, gratified that they were working as a team despite the lack of real rehearsal time. It was the mark of true professionals.

A sudden movement on the firing line, and Uri hesitated, grim smile faltering, the field glasses up and scanning for a better view. The courier was *moving*, dammit, snaking out from cover now, as if deliberately deciding to expose himself. Another heartbeat, and the carload of gunners would have him in their sights.

Nosenko saw the movement coming, watched the American soldier's arm swing up and out, releasing the grenade—and he could not believe his eyes. He fumbled with the radio, about to shout a warning, but the lethal egg had disappeared beneath the backup vehicle, and by then it was too late.

The dark sedan erupted into boiling flame, the hood and trunk springing open like an alligator's jaws. Nosenko half imagined he could hear his soldiers screaming inside there, knew it had to be impossible; he closed his mind to it. A dancing, burning figure staggered from the car and traveled half a dozen steps before a rifle bullet knocked him sprawling.

Uri felt his stomach turning over; he had to swallow hard to keep its contents down. He saw his plan disintegrating right before his eyes, and for the first time in his life he was uncertain how he should respond.

There was a chance, if he could reach the killing ground in time. A chance that he could organize a final rush and overrun the soldier, bury him beneath a final blitz. Retrieval of the ransom was a secondary problem now, impossible before the enemy was vanquished.

Uri made his move, already turning from the window as he finished ticking off alternatives.

His reputation, no, life itself was riding on the outcome of this firefight. He could not afford defeat. Illyanovich would never accept excuses from a trained professional. Failure would be punished. Illyanovich was accustomed only to success.

Nosenko decided that he would keep his record clean if it cost the life of every soldier in his troop.

He reached the narrow stairs and took them in a rush. The Mauser automatic was in his hand and ready. A dozen strides along a dingy corridor, and he was on the street, surrounded by the sounds and smell of combat.

It was worse than he had dared imagine.

Fully half his force was down and out of

action, killed or wounded by the courier's precision bursts. Along the sidewalk, huddled bodies lay like so much rubbish, streams and pools of blood imparting color to the pavement. Uri started counting; he stopped, disgusted, when he got to nine.

Moving out of cover, he was tracking onto target with the Mauser as the quarry showed himself, already squeezing off a rapid double-punch. The empty casings arced across his line of vision, rattled on the sidewalk at his feet.

And suddenly, the human target was no longer there. Nosenko recognized the error within a heartbeat. A dozen paces to his left, the enemy was rising, coming up and out of a well-practiced shoulder roll, his small submachine gun leveled, winking flame.

The stunning impact was like a giant fist smashing through his rib cage. Pain seared. Nosenko felt his knees give way. The ground raced up to meet him. There was no pain with that final impact, only numbness and a deep, pervasive chill.

Dying, he marveled at the ease with which it happened, felt the power ebbing from him, dribbling out to join the other pools and rivulets that marked the sidewalk. A memory of Stalingrad, and snow, arrived unbidden. . .the frigging Nazis were everywhere, but Uri had the patience to outlast them all. Hard reality unraveled like a skein of yarn in his failing mind, leaving a black space much blacker even than the darkest moments of the last great war.

APRIL ROSE CHECKED THE WEAPON in her lap.

The American 180 automatic carbine was special. Deceptively light, the rifle held 177 rounds of .22 hollowpoint ammunition in a drum mounted flat atop the slim receiver. In full-automatic mode, the gun could generate a cyclic rate of 1,800 rounds per minute, shredding human targets with grisly efficiency. A Laser Lok sight, mounted horizontally beneath the barrel, eliminated the need to sight or aim, making any miss a virtual impossibility at ranges of 200 yards and more.

And she would need the firepower, every ounce of it.

At the first sound of shooting she was EVA, flicking off her weapon's safety and activating the laser sight.

As she reached the corner, April found a battle raging in the street around the Café Vittorio. Perhaps a dozen snipers had the restaurant besieged, pouring fire from automatic rifles through the shattered windows. A car blazed at the curb.

She saw Bolan crawling, squeezing off

short, selective bursts from his machine pistol. Gunners on the street were seeking cover, dodging into doorways of adjacent shops or crouching behind parked cars. One of them, positioned on the roof above a tailor's shop, was coming dangerously close with rounds from his assault rifle.

April snapped the autocarbine to her shoulder and let the laser beam reach out and find the target. At 100 yards, the red spot was two inches wide and centered under the sniper's outstretched arm.

She stroked the trigger, ripping off a dozen rounds in half a second. There was no recoil—merely a sensation of the rifle's power—and the hollowpoint manglers were on target, shredding flesh and vital organs into bloody pulp. The sniper dropped his rifle, did an awkward pirouette as he tumbled backward off the roof.

April dropped her sights. She scanned for another target. She picked out a rifleman emerging from the doorway of a clothing store. The laser death-beam settled on his upper lip. She held the trigger down for a full second and watched face and skull disintegrate into a crimson spray. The headless body staggered, finally sprawled across the sidewalk.

A handgunner had spotted her and was

swinging into target acquisition when she hit him with a burst that tore his arm off at the shoulder.

A screech of brakes alerted her to danger at her back. April spun around to find a dark sedan approaching, doors springing open, releasing troops. Half a dozen hard-men were closing on her, pistols cocked and ready.

She swung the 180 around and into action, bringing the blinding laser beam into the nearest gunner's eyes. Before he could react, the bullets followed, drilling through his face and forehead, the impact lifting him off his feet and slamming him against the car.

April held the trigger down, raking across the car from left to right, watching tiny holes appear in doors and windshields. Startled troops were ducking, scrambling for cover; one of them, a shade too slow, was blown away and out of the laser's view.

Pistols were cracking, bullets whining past her.

She felt a blow at her side, followed instantly by searing pain.

She was losing her balance, falling.

The autocarbine spun from her grasp.

Another blinding flash exploded in her skull. It gave way to darkness, bottomless and cold.

BOLAN DROPPED A CARELESS SNIPER with the Uzi's final burst. He reloaded on the run, still ducking scattered incoming rounds. He had cut the odds against him by about a third.

A rifle bullet chipped the pavement near his foot. Bolan answered with a burst that blew the gunner backward through the broad front window of a store. Alarm bells joined the hellish background chorus.

The Executioner was looking for another angle of attack when he recognized the sound of April's autorifle.

He saw a dying sniper plunging off the roof across the street. Then a second gunner dropped. Then a third. Helpful little .22s were sweeping them away, clearing a corridor for his escape.

He was up and moving toward her when he saw the enemy sedan slide to a halt against the curb behind her.

Men were piling out and rushing at her, but she heard them coming and turned to face the threat.

She took the nearest soldier's head off, knocked another sprawling with a burst of hollowpoints, peppering the car as she retreated.

A revolver answered, swiftly joined by others, rapid fire converging on the slender target.

Then April staggered.

And Bolan saw the blood, bright and terrible against the fabric of her jump suit. The terrorists were still unloading at her as she sprawled against a lamp post.

Snarling out his rage, Bolan held the Uzi's trigger down, hosing the enemy with hot steel-jacketed parabellums. Men were dying under fire. Bolan saw a pair go down in a single thrashing heap. Others were scrambling for safety in the car, abandoning their target on the street corner.

Bolan heard the engine of the dark sedan revving up, the wheelman coming off his mark with smoking tires. The driver and the gunners wanted to gut Bolan. They raced down the street toward the Café Vittorio.

Bolan seized a frag grenade from the rapidly decreasing store hidden around the inside of his jacket. He pulled the pin and let the grenade fly, counting into the pitch. At twenty yards he made the toss, leading the sedan and estimating range with accuracy born of practice. The grenade bounced once on the vehicle's shiny hood and detonated a foot above the windshield. The car swerved sharply, tried to climb the bumper of another car, then came to rest, one of its front wheels free of any contact with the crumpled metal of the vehicles' mating and spinning uselessly in the air.

Beyond the wreckage, Bolan saw a pair of riflemen retreating at a gallop. He chased them with a burst from the Uzi, dropping both in a sprawl on the pavement.

Silence fell across the battlefield, broken only by muffled whimpering from inside the restaurant and the brittle sound of glass dropping out of shattered window frames.

Bolan took off across the street. He reached the car that had terminally mounted the other and looked in through a shattered window. The car was full of dying men, two slumped in the front, others jumbled together in a heap in the back. Gasoline was dribbling from the ruptured tank and fuel line, filling the air with fumes.

One of the bodies at the back stirred, moaning from the pain of the body-rupturing collision. Bolan grabbed a handful of bloody hair, twisted hard to get the guy's complete attention.

"Who are you working for?" he asked, cold eyes cutting into the guy's last moments.

The hardman was struggling to get the answer out.

"Go...hell...."

Bolan reached into his pants pocket and pulled out a cigarette lighter. He flicked it with his thumb. He slowly moved the flame toward the evaporating pool of gasoline.

"One more time," he grated. "Let's have a name."

The wounded soldier's eyes had widened with terror, weak defiance leaking out of him along with vital fluids.

It was the terror that killed him. Bolan had to strain his ears to catch the last words the guy would ever speak.

"Twenty miles north...old military base...Paradine."

Bolan let the guy die. He ran like hell. He ran to leave death behind him and find life. Life in the ruins. *April must live*!

15

BOLAN FOUND APRIL'S PULSE and held it, counting off the vital numbers. Her lifeline was weak, erratic.

She moaned, shifting on the bunk and grimacing against the pain. She was feverish, verging on delirium. Bolan had controlled the bleeding with battlefield first aid. The Executioner had done his best, but April needed more than his medical efforts.

The surrounding countryside was cloaked in darkness, gently rolling meadowland obscured by the moonless night. Bolan had the Laser Wagon's homing beacon tuned to a preselected frequency; special high-beam infrareds illuminated their position, making out a makeshift helipad for those with special eyes to see.

He saw the chopper coming, following his beacon, long before he heard the engines. The Huey's running lights were golden embers in the darkness, drawing closer almost imperceptibly until they were upon him.

The pilot was equipped with special head-gear, permitting him to navigate on Bolan's infrared landing lights. He brought the ungainly airship down on target. Rotors slowed, finally stopped as the pilot let the engines idle, keeping them warm and ready for lift-off.

Paramedics were the first to disembark, two men carrying a stretcher furled between them. Bolan looked all around for potential aggravation; midnight maneuvers would not be treated lightly by local authorities. Then his eyes caught the figure slowly emerging from the helicopter.

Hal Brognola looked as if he had aged a dozen years since that morning. His face was drawn and haggard, his broad shoulders stooped under an invisible burden. Bolan waited for his longtime friend beside the Laser Wagon.

"You didn't do this, Hal," he said. "It's not your fault."

Brognola was trying to light a cigar, having trouble with his matches. "Was it Paradine, do you know?"

"Affirmative."

"You got a fix on him?"

Bolan nodded. "I had a heart-to-heart with one of his troops. There's an old military installation twenty miles north."

The paramedics were emerging from the Laser Wagon bearing April on the stretcher. She had been sedated. They took her swiftly to the waiting chopper and disappeared inside. Bolan watched the scene.

The medivac chopper was about to carry a major portion of his life away from him.

Perhaps forever.

WITH A SUPREME EFFORT, the mercenary chief restrained himself. His voice was ice.

"I want to know what happened, Michael."

The other man shifted uncomfortably in his chair. Paradine looked as if he was about to explode into violence.

"An ambush of some kind. It looks like our people got caught in the middle."

"Survivors?"

"Unknown. GIS has the town sewn up tight."

"And Phoenix?"

Michael spread his hands in a helpless gesture. "I told you—"

"*Nothing!*" Paradine detonated, standing up so quickly that the seated man shrank back involuntarily. Paradine began circling the small command hut like a caged predator at feeding time.

"You were surprised at Monte Carlo," he

sneered. "The trouble at Udine may have been the Red Brigades. Now, we lose an entire crew, and it's a mystery?"

The lieutenant steeled himself to speak with candor.

"How are we supposed to find him if he missed his contact? And what about the woman?"

"Enough," Paradine hissed. "I ask for answers and you give me foolish questions. Phoenix will find *us*, whether we like it or not. It's your job to be ready for him when he comes."

Michael was regarding Paradine with cautious incredulity.

"We need to waste the hostages," he said. "It's crazy to sit around and wait."

Paradine smashed him in the face with his open palm. The blow knocked the lieutenant out of his chair and onto the floor. Paradine towered over him, eyes blazing, one hand locked around the butt of his holstered Browning automatic.

"I want the compound on full alert, beginning immediately! No one sleeps or leaves his post for any reason. Double up around the perimeter."

Michael struggled to his feet and backed out of the room.

Paradine, breathing heavily, returned to

his desk and slumped into the swivel chair. A pulse was throbbing in his temple.

His lieutenant had been right. There was a great risk in waiting any longer at the compound. But he would not let anything divert him from his course now.

Paradine had come to know his adversary, could recognize his strengths and weaknesses. He was certain his enemy would recognize the ransom message for exactly what it was.

A personal challenge.

16

THE EXECUTIONER HAD LONG AGO prepared himself for death in battle. It was not defeatist thinking, but a rational acceptance of the inevitable. Even everlasting war must have an ending for the individual combatant, and no warrior was invincible. He could prolong the struggle, live to fight another day if he was strong enough, skillful enough, but in the end, Death was the the undefeated champion of every war.

Certain skilled professionals had attached themselves to Mack Bolan's crusade and made it theirs. But Bolan sought no allies in his war. The door was always open if any of his people chose to leave. He would not think less of any of them for seeking another way of living.

Some who joined his war had paid the ultimate price for their involvement. They traveled with him now, in spirit, every mile along his odyssey.

The Executioner was not a dispassionate or

unemotional man, despite appearances. There was a hot, volcanic rage simmering beneath the cool exterior. The war was personal to Bolan. Despite the foreign names and global issues, he was never able to truly divorce the heart and mind. It was the heart that led him into his crusade. He had sworn an oath from the heart when he stood over the open graves of his mother, father, sister. It was the heart as well as the mind that kept him fighting.

In Vietnam, the same spirit had led him to risk his life transporting wounded villagers— even injured adversaries—through the lines.

But there would be no mercy for his enemies tonight. Only full eradication would satisfy him now.

17

BOLAN SET THE LASER WAGON'S parking brake and killed the engine. He pulled down the miniature viewing screen of his laser-optic spotting scope, turning on and tuning in a greenish-tinted picture of the surrounding landscape.

He was parked on a slight rise, amid the only large trees within 200 yards. In front of him, the land fell away, sloping gently, leveling off in grassy plains a half mile distant. At the foot of the slope, Bolan's spotting screen picked out the dark images of towers and buildings clustered together.

He fine-tuned the magnification until the cluster, separated from him by a moonless half mile, looked as though it was a hundred yards away at twilight. He could count the buildings, pick out human figures in the wooden towers, see the figures that moved back and forth across open areas in edgy protection of a hardsite that simmered dangerously in a dangerous night.

Bolan marked the buildings of the site—two long barracks, either of them big enough to hold the hostages; the smaller CO's quarters; other sheds for storage, communications, the compound's generator.

He could make out from the lighted windows of the generator hut the web of heavy-duty cables radiating from its roof. Klieg lights were mounted on the tower observation post, but were unlit.

Bolan reached forward and tripped the Fire Enable switch on his command console. Above and behind him, he heard the whirring of machinery as the hidden rocket pod was elevated, rising through retracted roof panels, locking into readiness. The system, duplicated with improvements from Bolan's first War Wagon gave the Executioner a four-punch capability at ranges of a mile and more.

The new vehicle would be tested by fire; its baptism would be in flaming war. Bolan did not prefer to roadtest the Laser Wagon quite so cruelly, but circumstances were dictating his choices. Just as radar was discovered to meet the needs of the Second World War, Stony Man Farm's new product had to be force-grown in the hothouse of history. Later he could stash the wagon in a secure place and check it over at his leisure; it was still only in prototyle form, to be developed over time, and he looked forward to getting involved with it away from the battlefield.

In front of him, grid lines appeared on the viewing screen as it became a range finder with direct connections to the battlewagon's firing system. Any target held at center screen received an instant readout of range and elevation, allowing Bolan to lock the firebirds onto preselected marks with pinpoint accuracy. Within the limits of the system, he could hit anything the laser optics let him see.

He focused on a guard tower, waited for the luminous display of range, then hit the Target Acquisition button. On the console, pulsing scarlet letters told him that Target No. 1 was registered and locked into the battlecruiser's data banks.

A second elevated guard post, at the opposite end of the hardsite, was the next target. A light machine gun faced inward from it onto the courtyard, and Bolan brought video cross hairs to rest on the gun mount. Target No. 2 also read into the data bank's memory.

Bolan panned the scope until the generator hut was framed at center screen. A fingertip against the Target Acquisition button, and another target locked into the rocketry programming circuits and was registered for hell.

There was one target remaining. Bolan focused on the motor pool, the cluster of jeeps and canvas-covered military trucks beside the CP. He chose one of the surplus eight-wheelers as his reference point, counting on its fuel reserve to do the rest as he keyed the acquisition mode for Target No. 4.

The Executioner could send his comets on their way immediately with a gentle rocking pressure on the floorboard firing pedal, but instead he waited. The rocketry was programmed to respond on cue and Bolan planned to be a good deal closer to his target when the fireworks erupted.

The laser-optic rocketry was his back up system only, and he meant to use it for diversionary purposes. Without a close reconnaissance, he could not afford to blast the barracks or Paradine's command post.

He left the console and moved back along the battlewagon's length to armory and living quarters, scrutinizing the equipment as he did so. He readied himself for the battle to come by absorbing his mind in the hardware. His eyes lighted on the satchel of diamonds.

Bolan ignored it—never did he plan on negotiation, he would just use the stones to get through the checkpoints.

If there was any negotiating to be done, the Executioner would do it with a gun.

PARADINE RESTLESSLY CIRCLED THE SITE, checking his sentries and making certain they were alert and ready. He did not waste time trying to describe Phoenix or his style of fighting. You could not explain a cyclone of death.

Initially Paradine had wished for time to gather better troops. His mercenaries were experienced and dedicated to a point, but they were accustomed to wars of hit and run, wars where the targets were usually unarmed, incapable of striking back. He wondered how they would do in open battle when confronted with an enemy like Phoenix.

He reached the eastern guard tower and scrambled up a wooden ladder to the platform twenty feet above his head. The two guards standing watch were silent as Paradine climbed through a trapdoor. He ignored them, moving to the railing and staring across the darkened landscape.

Phoenix was out there somewhere, waiting, watching, biding his time. Paradine could feel his presence.

An idea struck him with elemental force. He knew exactly what would bring his adversary in...and on the run, making the canny warrior careless in his haste.

BOLAN WAS IN BLACKSUIT and rigged for war, his face and hands darkened with combat cosmetics. The Beretta 93-R was in its honored place, tucked into breakaway shoulder leather. The mini-Uzi rode his hip in military rigging, ready to meet fire with fire.

The side arms and their extra magazines were loaded with Glaser Safety Slugs, the latest in lethal ballistic technology. Behind the tip of every slug, a copper jacket held pellets of No. 12 shot suspended in liquid Teflon. The projectiles were designed to exit from the muzzle at tremendous speeds, smash into the target and release their shot with stunning force. In living flesh, the results were devastating.

The Glasers had another built-in advantage made to order for the warrior's needs. The slugs could never ricochet, to accidentally kill or maim the innocent. At close quarters, on uncertain ground with hostages at risk, Bolan would be thankful for the special edge the Glasers gave him.

His head weapon for the probe was the hybrid over-under M-16/M-203 combination, an assault rifle capable of spewing deadly 5.56mm tumblers at a cyclic rate of 700 rpm in automatic mode, while supplemented by a 40mm launcher attached beneath the barrel.

Belts crossing Bolan's chest contained a preselected mix of 40mm high-explosive, gas and buckshot rounds, arranged for swift availability in combat.

The soldier took a final inventory of his doomsday rigging—stilettos and garrotes in hidden pockets, grenades and the radio-remote detonator on his web belt, extra magazines for all his weapons. Satisfied, he shouldered an O.D. satchel filled with plastic charges and put the Laser Wagon behind him. Outside in the cool air, the friendly dark enveloped him.

Bolan made his way silently across the landscape, following the terraces downslope toward Paradine. He tested the night, combat senses probing, alert for any signs of danger.

He was 300 yards from target when the hardsite came alive. Every light inside the wire perimeter was suddenly ablaze, the courtyard illuminated noonday-bright. In the guard towers, klieg lights blazed into light, their dazzling beams directed down into the center of the camp.

From his vantage point on the hillside,

Bolan saw the installation as an amphitheater. The center stage was being prepared for a surprise command performance.

Something big was about to happen.

A death drama.

18

BOLAN FLATTENED HIMSELF against the turf, thirty feet outside the installation's perimeter. There were sentries on the wire, spaced at hundred-foot intervals, but they—like their high-rise counterparts in the gun towers—all seemed more intent on what was about to happen in the courtyard. Bolan edged closer. He kept one hand tight around the assault rifle.

Terrorists were shouting inside the camp. Bolan heard languages mingling in a grim cacophony.

He saw his target. Standing off to one side, watching the proceedings and sizing up his troops in action, Paradine was dressed exactly as he had been when the Executioner saw him last. In black. Mirrored aviator shades were in place. An AK-47 was suspended muzzle down from a leather strap across his shoulder.

It would be an easy shot from Bolan's position. A single tumbler from the M-16 could do the job, or he could stroke the trigger of his M-203 and drop a high-explosive can on top of Paradine. So simple.

Caution stayed his hand, and Bolan killed the temptation. If Paradine was hit, the hostages would be open game.

As he watched, the prisoners came trooping through a barracks entrance to his right, flanked by riflemen who herded them in single file across open space. Bolan counted sixteen, with a stewardess and two men in airline uniforms bringing up the rear.

The hostages were jostled and prodded by the terrorists into a huddled clutch at center stage. Spotlights pinned them, rifles with nervous fingers on the triggers surrounded them. Any sudden move would spark a firestorm.

The Executioner was moving, circling, ducking in to place a charge against the fence and backing off again to the shelter of the darkness. He repeated the procedure every hundred feet, until his circuit of the preoccupied installation was complete and he was back where he had started.

The plastic charges were implanted with time-delay detonators, keyed to Bolan's radio-remote control. With the box at his waist, he could blow them all together, or in opposing pairs, or in rapid-fire succession with two-second lag time between the blasts.

He was here to teach them all to fear the Phoenix fire.

Paradine stood before the hostages like a general preparing to address his troops.

The gunners flanking Paradine carried Kalashnikovs.

Out beyond the lights, Bolan prepared to make his move.

SARAH SHEPHERD HAD JERKED ERECT, snapping out of a light sleep, momentarily forgetting where she was. She felt an urge to scream, but fought it, swallowing the sudden surge of panic. The pain inside her skull returned in nauseating waves, answered by a throbbing in her wounded side.

Something had awakened her—a sound. She heard voices, and....

The door burst open and a gang of Arab guards stormed into the barracks, jostling and prodding at the hostages, barking unintelligible orders in their native language. Ranging up and down the Quonset's barren length, they herded everyone together, striking out at stragglers with their rifle butts.

A solitary figure filled the barracks door, and Sarah recognized the tall American as one of those who had accompanied the blond leader on the 747. He had changed from his business suit to mottled camouflage and pistol belt. The rifle in his hands was identical to those the Arabs carried.

When he reached the center of the hut, the mercenary halted, standing in a circle of expectant, nervous hostages.

"We're moving out," he said. "I want you all in the yard in single file. Paradine will give you your instructions there."

Paradine. The name was unfamiliar to her, but fitting—cold and bloodless, like the man himself—and it cut across her nerves like a razor.

Sarah braced against the corrugated-metal wall, then struggled to her feet, gasping at the sudden spasm of pain caused by injured ribs. A momentary wave of dizziness enveloped her, but quickly passed.

The hostages were filing out, and Sarah fell in line.

Outside, the compound was bright as day with every light ablaze. Mercenaries stood facing the line of hostages. Sarah caught a fleeting glimpse of snipers in the towers overhead, their automatic weapons following the short procession.

Ahead of her, the prisoners were stumbling to a halt, the line folding into a clump of dazed, helpless people. Sarah tried to find the center of the group to surround herself with people. She was desperate for a place to hide, a way to make herself invisible.

The lady was no longer frightened. She was terrified.

She knew instinctively that there was something wrong. Suddenly breathless with fear, she felt she might suffocate.

The mercenary leader, Paradine, was watching from the sidelines, another pair of uniformed Americans behind him. His silvered glasses caught the light and reflected it like coals of fire, giving his face a grim, Satanic look.

She was in the presence of the damned, and Sarah knew there was no escape.

The man in black began to speak. His voice was a monotone that belied the menace of his words.

"Your governments have chosen to ignore my terms," he said. "In view of their reluctance, I am left with no choice."

Sarah heard the calm, hideous pronouncement of her death. Now she was ready to fight. Now Sarah Shepherd wanted to live.

They were surrounded, pinned beneath the searchlights with nowhere to run.

Paradine was backing off. His voice rose, reaching out to gunmen ranged around the camp's perimeter. He barked commands in Arabic, repeated them in German and Italian, watched as the mercenaries closed their ring around the hostages. Rifle bolts snapped back and forth. The sound was the gnashing teeth of savage machinery.

Sarah Shepherd stood strong and prayed.

"Ready!"

Paradine glared at the huddled captives.

"Aim!"

The night erupted into thunder. The mercenary leader recoiled from the blast.

Phoenix had struck.

The western tower crumpled and collapsed in flaming ruins.

A fiery comet streaked across the compound, impacting on the eastern tower at Paradine's back.

A ball of fire devoured the observation deck of the tower, consuming startled troops before they had a chance to scream. Then the legs of the tower blew outward and the platform dropped heavily to earth, expelling smoke and cinders in a blinding cloud.

Michael passed Paradine on the run, shouting at the troops and calling them to order. Some of them responded sluggishly, but most were busy scrambling to protect themselves, seeking any cover they could find. Along the fence, an automatic rifle opened up, the gunner firing into empty darkness, and another quickly joined the chorus.

Paradine dismissed them from his mind. He did not care if they killed each other pursuing shadows. Phoenix was his only concern, and he was ready to receive the enemy.

He primed the folding-stock Kalashnikov and released its safety. He was moving, looking for a safe position with a field of fire, when another rocket hurtled overhead, homing on the generator shack. Paradine saw the Quonset hut disintegrate. Cables snaked wildly off in all directions as the camp blacked out.

Somewhere on his flank, a woman screamed. Male voices, frightened, angry, were cursing at the sudden darkness. Around the camp's perimeter, a score of weapons stuttered into life.

There was still a chance, if he could reach the truck park. The vehicles could give him light and hope, bring order out of milling chaos. He veered hard left, running now at full speed.

Navigating by the firelight, he made directly for the trucks, ignoring the running figures as they brushed past him. One of the Egyptian hostages stumbled to a halt in front of him, and Paradine swung his rifle barrel in a vicious arc, connecting with a startled face. Paradine charged on.

He was thirty yards from target when a

meteor descended on the truck park, detonating beneath the cab of a military eight-wheeler. The truck reared up, riding on a tongue of oily flame before it went to pieces. The truck park became a boiling lake of fire. Fuel tanks were going off in quick succession, a volcanic string of fireworks. The concussion slammed Paradine to the earth.

He hugged the ground and felt the panic rising in him as it had in Turkey and in his nightmares. The trembling began in his stomach, radiated outward into his limbs. He gripped the AK-47 tighter, willing himself to rise and fight.

The nightmares were over now for Paradine, replaced by grim reality, his second chance at Phoenix. The last chance for the terrorist mercenary to redeem himself, or die.

"YOUR GOVERNMENTS HAVE CHOSEN to ignore my terms. In view of their reluctance, I am left with no choice."

Crouching on the edge of darkness, Bolan listened to the death sentence and saw the troops prepare to open fire upon hearing Paradine's command. It was a trap, the mercenary's last and most desperate ploy to draw him out, but for Bolan there was no time for weighing odds and angles.

He found the radio-remote control by

touch and keyed the rocketry for single fire.
Bolan counted down the heartbeats, reaching five before a hurtling comet filled his
peripheral vision, homing on the western guard tower, slamming between the
spindly legs. The lookout post disintegrated
with a resounding thunderclap, propelling
guards, guns and shattered lumber into a
free-fall.

Mass confusion broke out, hearts racing,
pumping, guns pumping, the hostages forgotten as their captors turned to face the outer
perimeters. Paradine was in a combat crouch,
his flankers fanning out to cover him, but the
rank and file were still groping toward a recognition of the true threat.

Before the first retaliatory round was fired,
Bolan had punched the key again and was
watching a second firebird crackle in from
downrange, taking out the second tower in a
roaring ball of flame.

The eruption splintered wood and turned
shards into sleek missiles. Hot shock waves
fractured the air and laid waste the earth. A
driving firerain of destruction ripped apart
dreams as it tore open guts, broke heads,
snapped limbs. Nearby survivors continued
to pump weapons into the night, seeking nonexistent targets. Distant troops scrambled
away from whatever they thought would be

the next target; they fled from the carnage to come.

Bolan launched another rocket, and in split seconds the hardsite's generator went to hell, blacking out the camp and pitching already terrified mercenaries into dark horror. Fire along the fence increased. Bolan hugged the earth, avoiding strays.

In front of him, the midnight landscape had acquired a reddish hue, firelight casting mottled shadows on the huts and running figures.

He saw the prisoners, led by a woman, breaking for freedom. Terrorists were firing in the darkness, wildly, aimlessly, at every phantom they thought they saw or heard.

Bolan had to penetrate the enemy camp before the rattled troops recovered from their panic.

He spotted Paradine, a dodging, weaving figure, in the fire-bright smoke, minus flankers now. He was running across the killing ground. Paradine was making for the truck park.

Bolan saw the enemy's intention. He then stroked the radio-remote and dispatched his final fireball. Paradine was closing on his target when a blast obliterated the middle of the truck park, spewing fiery streamers of gasoline in all directions. The explosion top-

pled Paradine, and Bolan lost sight of him
as secondary blasts devoured the trucks and
jeeps, laying down a pall of oily smoke.

It was time to move. Bolan was on his
feet and leaping forward when he keyed
the time-delay plastique for rapid-fire se-
quential detonation. Starting on his left
and moving counterclockwise, a string of
giant firecrackers tore the night apart,
marching right around the compound and
opening a dozen gaps in Paradine's defensive line.

It would take a strong, coordinated force
to close them all, and at the moment, Paradine was on his own.

Bolan hit the trigger of his M-203, dropping a can of high explosive into the command hut. He saw the corrugated-metal
structure ripple, bulge, before it went to
pieces with a numbing roar. Disintegrating
roofs and walls became jagged pieces of steel
impacting flesh as mercenaries scrambled for
another sanctuary.

At the wire, Bolan found an opening and
slipped into Paradine's defensive ring. Terrorists and prisoners were everywhere, charg-
ing through the fire and dust in a desperate
search for exits.

Few of the gunners held their posts, but a
handful of stoic Germans stood at some of

the smoking gaps to hold them and prevent troops or hostages breaking out.

Two of these hardguys saw Bolan and accosted him, weapons swinging up and onto target. The Executioner responded with his M-16, hammering a figure eight that blew them both away. He was moving, seeking other targets, as their bodies hit the ground.

Bolan was in, but the battle was far from over.

He advanced across the killing ground, a lethal specter shielded by the drifting battle smoke. The Executioner was on a dragon hunt.

The dragon was Paradine.

19

BOLAN FED A CANISTER OF GAS into his 40mm
thunder-gun and sent it downrange to join the
battle smoke. Tracking on, he swung the
stubby launcher and released another gas
round, spreading the hellish cloud over friend
and foe. The choking fumes did not dis-
criminate.

Bolan had to keep the terrorists off guard,
confused, reeling, jumping at their shadows.
It was a risky game, especially for the milling
hostages, but he had to play the cards as they
were dealt.

He saved the automatic rifle for precision
work, spending single rounds and short, selective bursts when targets came into view.
He toppled six terrorists without revealing his
position. He kept moving, hunting Paradine.

The mercenary had obviously found himself a hole.

Bolan slipped an HE can into the launcher's breech and locked it down, pivoting in
the direction of the nearest barracks. Firing

from the hip, he dropped the round through the Quonset's open window, backing off before it detonated.

The barracks seemed to swell, straining at the seams, before a blinding bubble of flame ripped it apart. The roof was sent skyward, riding on a tongue of fire, furniture and fixtures sucked along behind it. Smoking walls crumpled.

Bolan reloaded on the run, moving toward the other barracks before the dust and ash had settled from the first blast. Thirty yards from his target, he stroked the launcher's trigger, riding out the recoil and watching as the installation's final standing structure rocked, disintegrated. A rising scream was muffled, snuffed out by the hungry crackle of the flames.

Across the compound, Paradine's American terrorists were rallying survivors, desperately trying to collect a fighting force. A handful of men were responding.

One of the guncocks spotted Bolan. The Americans were leading out, firing 7.62mm hornets as they came.

Bolan hit a long shoulder roll, coming out of it a dozen yards west of his original position. Kneeling, he chambered a 40mm round of buckshot, placing a finger on the launcher's trigger as his opposition closed the gap.

A rapid scan revealed an open field of fire, and Bolan spent a couple of precious seconds searching for the hostages. His eyes caught a young woman herding a group of them through the ruptured fence behind the motor pool, and the warrior wished them well. They were bound for life. The Executioner was occupied with death.

A bullet smacked the earth beside his knee, another tugged at his sleeve. Bolan turned his full attention to the enemy. He met them at a range of forty yards with fire and lead, twenty of the deadly double-ought pellets slicing into flesh and vital organs. One of the Americans was disemboweled, a pair of Palestinians behind him ventilated, blown away.

Bolan tracked them, scanning with his automatic rifle. He stitched a line of tumblers along the trailing flank, dropping half a dozen hardguys in thrashing, screaming agony. Another burst, and they were silent, deathly still.

Two terror-mercs were left with Bolan on the hellgrounds. They were slick, professional, peeling off in opposite directions, laying down a covering barrage. Angry steel-jackets filled the air, snapping past Bolan's face and giving lethal substance to the night.

Bolan took the soldier on his left, hanging a wreath of tumblers around his neck with surgical precision. The mercenary's skull exploded, a bloody fountain pumping in the firelight, before his body toppled over into dusty death.

The second trooper had his target marked and measured, squeezing off a burst that could have sectioned Bolan at the waist—but Bolan had moved. The Executioner was flat on the ground to one side, his rifle automatically swinging into bull's-eye acquisition. With a gentle squeeze, three rounds rattled off in automatic fire, and the mercenary sat down hard, dark blood soaking through his jacket just above the heart.

Bolan scrambled to his feet, snapped another magazine into the M-16 and moved out.

He had a rendezvous to keep.

PARADINE WAS TRAPPED inside a nightmare, overpowered by a numbing sense of déjà vu. He roamed the killing ground in search of Phoenix, half afraid of finding him. The stench of death and burning rubble filled his nostrils.

It was Turkey all over again, but worse. The mercenary's trap was being turned against him. He felt the jaws about to close around his throat.

He passed the broken bodies of his soldiers as he prowled. Vacant, sightless eyes observed him with disdain. They were dead, finished, but the game went on for Paradine, and he was losing. If he did not find Phoenix soon, he was afraid his nerve might break.

A German, one of his Baader-Meinhof rejects, stumbled into view, his pallid face streaked with blood. The shaken, dazed terrorist approached Paradine, moving like a zombie in the firelit night.

Paradine, feeling no pity for the beaten man, raised his AK-47, finger tensing on the trigger, and squeezed off a burst. The stream of bullets knocked his human target backward, mauling flesh and fabric, casting him away, a floppy rag-doll figure with its stuffing falling out.

The sudden violence brought meager exhilaration to Paradine, releasing only a measure of the tension he was feeling. If he met the shadow warrior now, this minute. . . .

A tall figure, dressed in black and hung with weapons, was approaching through the battle haze. Paradine was jolted by the sight. Cold sweat beaded on his forehead. The shock of recognition was like a sharp blow to the heart.

It was Phoenix, cold and grim as death—a specter straight from Paradine's recurring dreams. He could have sketched the figure from his memory, supplied the smallest detail with his eyes closed.

A rifle stuttered on the dark perimeter, another chimed in, and Phoenix swiveled toward the sound. Without breaking stride, he launched a high-explosive shell in the direction of his enemies. The blast eclipsed the sniper fire and replaced it with ragged screams.

Paradine's Kalashnikov shuddered in his shaking hand, roared, and a stream of empty casings rattled at the mercenary's feet. Downrange, Phoenix staggered, stumbled, fell. In the blink of an eye he was down. He was on his back.

Paradine lowered the smoking rifle. Phoenix had fallen. Paradine had killed the warrior who stalked his dreams, the man who had put him through hell in Turkey.

Revenge.

Paradine pulled out his knife from its sheath—he wanted a souvenir. He wanted Phoenix's head.

MACK BOLAN LAY ON HIS BACK, immobile, registering pain and trying to arrive at a damage estimate. He felt the sticky warmth of blood against his side, below the arm, where a slug had burrowed in above the holstered Beretta. His chest and ribs were throbbing painfully, as if he had been struck repeatedly with leaded bats. It hurt to breathe.

His rifle had taken the brunt of it, stock and action shattered by a single round. He had taken the rest of it, his body pummeled by the rifle with an impact no less punishing than a projectile. He had to struggle for breath.

He took a rapid inventory, tensing one leg, then the other, moving on to arms and shoulders, waiting for the brittle pain of shattered bones. Everything was working.

Slowly, cautiously, the Executioner began to move. The right arm only, inching inward toward his side, the motion scarcely perceptible until his finger grazed the Uzi in its leather rigging at his hip. He felt the pistol grip and safety switch, the break-away release—and froze with his palm pressed flat against the holster.

Footsteps approached. Bolan's face was turned away. The gunner was closing on his blind side. There was no safe way to get a look at him.

The footsteps were a dozen paces out. Bolan gauged distance, estimated angles, tensed every muscle in his aching body. He would have to get it right the first time, for there would be no second chance. Mentally, he started counting down the numbers.

Like a lightning bolt, Bolan ripped the Uzi out of side leather, rolling over and sitting up and aiming in a single fluid motion. He was on the mark and squeezing off before he registered the face of his enemy, before he recognized the cruel mouth twisted in a silent snarl.

He held the Uzi's trigger down. Twenty Glasers rattled out in less than three seconds, dead on target. Paradine, thirty feet away, appeared to shiver, blur. He was dissolving where he stood. Emitting a noise made in hell, Paradine tumbled backward in death.

It was a grisly unbecoming that was over in an instant, and the mangled hulk of what had almost been a human being lay dead in the darkness.

Bolan slowly made it to his feet and fed the mini-gun another magazine. He flexed his shoulders and grimaced at the pain. He walked past the ravaged body of his enemy, refusing to look at the corpse. Anything remaining of the mercenary known as Paradine was harmless now, his menace grounded, drained away like so much static electricity.

Alone on the battlefield, Bolan felt the weight of ages on his shoulders. It threatened to pull him down. But war was the life that he had chosen, War Eternal, and it was too damned late to start having second thoughts about the course.

Resignedly, he shrugged off the weariness, the bruises, the ache of costly victory, and took himself away from the hellgrounds, going through the motions of a routine mop-up. There were hostages to gather in, the diamonds to return, and then, when he was finished, the soldier had a final stop to make.

EPILOGUE

"ONLY FOR A MINUTE, NOW. She needs her rest." The Air Force surgeon looked Bolan over with a more than casual interest and added, "You could stand some rest yourself."

"I'm getting there," the soldier told him.

Mack Bolan had never liked the antiseptic smell of hospitals. It reminded him of slow death, sluggish and cruel. Bolan put the morbid thought away and moved along the corridor in search of life.

Brognola waited for him outside Post-op, putting on a weary smile at the Executioner's approach. Bolan took his hand and wrung it warmly.

"The medics put her under, but they tell me that she's out of danger," Hal explained.

"I want to see her," Bolan said.

It was dark inside the private room, a dim light emanating from the door of the adjacent washroom. April occupied center stage, almost lost in the giant bed with its railings and assorted therapeutic hardware. An IV rig was fastened onto one side.

Bolan stood beside her in the semidarkness, captivated by the whisper of her breathing, the gentle rise and fall of the sheet across her breasts. There was something in his throat about to choke him.

The soldier reached out and lightly stroked her auburn hair. April shifted, murmured something underneath her breath. Her eyelids fluttered, finally opened.

"I knew you'd come," she said, her voice far off. "I've been waiting for you."

Bolan could say nothing. He looked at her, his jaw firm, his eyes warm.

"Can we go back home now?" she whispered.

"Soon," he told her. "Try to get some rest."

"You won't go without me?"

She was fading fast, the sedative reasserting its authority.

"I'll be right here."

"I love you."

She never heard his answer, but he told her anyway, bending down to brush her lips with his.

He found a chair against the wall, brought it over to her bedside and settled into it.

For the moment, he was done with war and

killing. It was respite, rather than reprieve. He knew there would be other battles, other enemies ahead. And the soldier and his lady would face them.

Together.

MACK BOLAN

THE EXECUTIONER 56

BOLAN

appears again in
Island Deathtrap

A foreign terrorist group has taken over a small island off the coast of Maine as a conduit for the importation of men and arms to the United States.

To ensure the secrecy of their hardsite, the criminals need the help of the local lobstermen and independent fishermen. The mob begins a campaign of terror aimed at the wives and families to "soften up" the boatmen.

Mack Bolan breaches the gang's defenses and becomes walking Death. He acts independently of Stony Man Farm to achieve his own kind of victory over hardship and combat stress in a new direction for this rogue warrior, who has always sought justice despite the enmity both of international crime and law enforcement.

MACK BOLAN

I am not their judge, I am their judgment—I am their executioner.
—*Mack Bolan,*
a.k.a. Col. John Phoenix

Mack Bolan is the free world's leading force in the new Terrorist Wars, defying all terrorists and destroying them piece by piece, using his Vietnam-trained tactics and knowledge of jungle warfare. Bolan's new war is the most exciting series ever to explode into print. You won't want to miss a single word. Start your collection now!

"This is a publishing marvel. Stores have a hard time keeping these books in stock!"
—*The Orlando Voice*

#39 The New War
#40 Double Crossfire
#41 The Violent Streets
#42 The Iranian Hit
#43 Return to Vietnam
#44 Terrorist Summit
#45 Paramilitary Plot
#46 Bloodsport

#47 Renegade Agent
#48 The Libya Connection
#49 Doomsday Disciples
#50 Brothers in Blood
#51 Vulture's Vengeance
#52 Tuscany Terror
#53 The Invisible Assassins
#54 Mountain Rampage

GOLD EAGLE

Available wherever paperbacks are sold.

Mack Bolan's

AN EXECUTIONER SERIES

ABLE TEAM

by Dick Stivers

In the fire-raking tradition of The Executioner, Able Team's Carl Lyons, Pol Blancanales and Gadgets Schwarz are the three hotshots who avenge terror with screaming silvered fury. They are the Death Squad reborn, and their long-awaited adventures are the best thing to happen since the Mack Bolan and the Phoenix Force series. Collect them all! They are classics of their kind! Do not miss these titles!

"This guy has a fertile mind and a great eye for detail. Dick Stivers is brilliant!"

—*Don Pendleton*

#1 Tower of Terror	#4 Amazon Slaughter
#2 The Hostaged Island	#5 Cairo Countdown
#3 Texas Showdown	#6 Warlord of Azatlan

Able Team titles are available wherever paperbacks are sold.

GOLD EAGLE

Mack Bolan's

PHOENIX FORCE

AN EXECUTIONER SERIES

by Gar Wilson

Phoenix Force is The Executioner's five-man army that blazes through the dirtiest of encounters. Like commandos who fight for the love of battle and the righteous unfolding of the logic of war, Bolan's five hardasses make mincemeat out of their enemies. Catch up on the whole series now!

"Strong-willed and true. Gold Eagle Books are making history. Full of adventure, daring and action!"

—*Marketing Bestsellers*

#1 **Argentine Deadline** #4 **Tigers of Justice**
#2 **Guerilla Games** #5 **The Fury Bombs**
#3 **Atlantic Scramble** #6 **White Hell**

Phoenix Force titles are available
wherever paperbacks are sold.

GOLD EAGLE

What readers are saying about Phoenix Force

"Sheer dynamite from cover to cover!"

—J.M.,* Dover, OH

"Superior reading—food for thought in every book! I can't wait for your next gut-crushers to hit the stands."

—M.C., Elmira, NY

"Your stories are so real they reach into the soul and touch chords some of us had forgotten."

—K.K., Westland, MI

"In every book I have learned a great deal, not only about tactics and weapons, but about the human character."

—J.S., Belleville, IL

"I love every action-packed minute!"

—R.D., Caneyville, KY

"Phoenix Force books are written with class."

—R.S., Tustin, CA

*Names available on request

HE'S EXPLOSIVE.
HE'S UNSTOPPABLE.
HE'S MACK BOLAN!

He learned his deadly skills in Vietnam...then put them to use by destroying the Mafia in a blazing one-man war. Now **Mack Bolan** is back to battle new threats to freedom, the enemies of justice and democracy—and he's recruited some high-powered combat teams to help. **Able Team**—Bolan's famous Death Squad, now reborn to tackle urban savagery too vicious for regular law enforcement. And **Phoenix Force**—five extraordinary warriors handpicked by Bolan to fight the dirtiest of anti-terrorist wars around the world.

Fight alongside these three courageous forces for freedom in all-new, pulse-pounding action-adventure novels! Travel to the jungles of South America, the scorching sands of the Sahara and the desolate mountains of Turkey. And feel the pressure and excitement building page after page, with nonstop action that keeps you enthralled until the explosive conclusion! Yes, Mack Bolan and his combat teams are living large...and they'll fight against all odds to protect our way of life!

Now you can have all the new Executioner novels delivered right to your home!

You won't want to miss a single one of these exciting new action-adventures. And you don't have to! Just fill out and mail the coupon following and we'll enter your name in the Executioner home subscription plan. You'll then receive four brand-new action-packed books in the Executioner series every other month, delivered right to your home! You'll get two **Mack Bolan** novels, one **Able Team** and one **Phoenix Force.** No need to worry about sellouts at the bookstore...you'll receive the latest books by mail as soon as they come off the presses. That's four enthralling action novels every other month, featuring all three of the exciting series included in The Executioner library. Mail the card today to start your adventure.

FREE! Mack Bolan bumper sticker.

When we receive your card we'll send your four explosive Executioner novels and, absolutely FREE, a Mack Bolan "Live Large" bumper sticker! This large, colorful bumper sticker will look great on your car, your bulletin board, or anywhere else you want people to know that you like to "Live Large." And you are under no obligation to buy anything—because your first four books come on a 10-day free trial! If you're not thrilled with these four exciting books, just return them to us and you'll owe nothing. The bumper sticker is yours to keep, FREE!

Don't miss a single one of these thrilling novels...mail the card now, while you're thinking about it. And get the Mack Bolan bumper sticker FREE!

BOLAN FIGHTS AGAINST ALL ODDS TO DEFEND FREEDOM

Mail this coupon today!

Gold Eagle Reader Service, a division of Worldwide Library
In U.S.A.: 2504 W. Southern Avenue, Tempe, Arizona 85282
In Canada: 649 Ontario Street, Stratford, Ontario N5A 6W2

FREE! MACK BOLAN BUMPER STICKER
when you join our home subscription plan.

YES. please send me my first four Executioner novels, and include my FREE
Mack Bolan bumper sticker as a gift. These first four books are mine to examine free fc
10 days. If I am not entirely satisfied with these books. I will return them within 10 day
and owe nothing. If I decide to keep these novels. I will pay just $1.95 per book (total
$7.80). I will then receive the four new Executioner novels every other month as soon
as they come off the presses. and will be billed the same low price of $7.80 per ship-
ment. I understand that each shipment will contain two Mack Bolan novels. one Able
Team and one Phoenix Force. There are no shipping and handling or any other hidden
charges. I may cancel this arrangement at any time. and the bumper sticker is mine to
keep as a FREE gift. even if I do not buy any additional books

NAME   (PLEASE PRINT)

ADDRESS   APT. NC

CITY   STATE/PROV.   ZIP/POSTAL COD

Signature   (If under 18. parent or guardian must sign.)

This offer limited to one order per household We reserve the right to exercise discretion in
granting membership If price changes are necessary. you will be notified Offer expires
December 31, 1983   166-BPM-PABE